DEFYING MR. DARNLEY

Augusta was outraged. How dare Robert Darnley of all men command her not to see Alfred de Hasard?

"You simply don't like him," Augusta declared. "*I* think he is very charming, and mean to receive him."

"Merely because you can write a fashionable trumpery novel, it does not make you *au courant* in the ways of the real world," Robert Darnley said, and moved to prove his point.

Augusta found her shoulders gripped by a pair of very strong hands, and a hungry mouth pressed against hers. She struggled, but her strength was no match for Darnley's—and after a few seconds, she was not certain that she wished it to be. But just as she ceased to struggle, he let go of her, strode away, and flung himself up onto his mount.

Trembling, Augusta shouted after him, "You are now and always were an odious, odious—*lout!*"

But he was out of earshot, and the wind carried her words toward the unlistening sea. . . .

A Signet Super Regency

"A tender and sensitive love story . . . an
exciting blend of romance and history"
—*Romantic Times*

The Guarded Heart
Barbara Hazard

Passion and danger embraced her—
but one man intoxicated her flesh
with love's irresistable promise . . .

Beautiful Erica Stone found her husband mysteriously murdered in Vienna and herself alone and helpless in this city
of romance . . . until the handsome, cynical Owen Kings-
ley, Duke of Graves, promised her protection if she would
spy for England among the licentious lords of Europe.
Aside from the danger and intrigue, Erica found herself
wrestling with her passion, for the tantalizingly reserved
Duke, when their first achingly tender kiss sparked a
desire in her more powerfully exciting than her hesitant
heart had ever felt before. . . .

A
SEA CHANGE

Caroline Brooks

A SIGNET BOOK

NEW AMERICAN LIBRARY

For Bunny

NAL BOOKS ARE AVAILABLE AT QUANTITY DISCOUNTS
WHEN USED TO PROMOTE PRODUCTS OR SERVICES
FOR INFORMATION PLEASE WRITE TO PREMIUM
MARKETING DIVISION, NEW AMERICAN LIBRARY, 1633
BROADWAY, NEW YORK, NEW YORK 10019.

Ⓢ SIGNET TRADEMARK REG. U.S.PAT. OFF AND FOREIGN COUNTRIES
REGISTERED TRADEMARK—MARCA REGISTRADA
HECHO EN CHICAGO, U.S.A.

SIGNET, SIGNET CLASSIC, MENTOR, ONYX, PLUME,
MERIDIAN and NAL BOOKS are published by NAL
PENGUIN INC., 1633 Broadway, New York, New York 10019

First Printing, December, 1987

1 2 3 4 5 6 7 8 9

PRINTED IN THE UNITED STATES OF AMERICA

1

To the casual observer, the lady seated at the delicate Queen Anne writing desk in the yellow silk morning room may have been the epitome of a fashionable ornament to Regency society, the ink drying on the nib of her pen as she gazed thoughtfully down into her spring garden and pondered the best way to call up an army of fashionable allies to attend a rout in a fortnight's time.

Certainly, there was nothing about her that would suggest anything of the bluestocking or a life spent more in pursuit of the intellect than the frivolous. From the points of lace on her very dashing cap, tied beneath one ear, through the morning dress confected from no less a modiste than Elvira in a froth of Brussels lace with ivory faggoting and a peplum hem deeply embroidered with oak leaves, acorns, and tassels, to the very tips of her ivory striped slippers, she seemed a lady of fashion.

But the eyes that stared blankly out the double windows, although of a pleasing teal, held a hint of shrewdness, and the mouth, although the lower lip was caught been a set of perfect teeth, betrayed a sense of levity, both qualitites frequently lacking in ladies who aspired to a life among the upper ten thousand.

As she glanced down at the paper on the blotter before her, it might have been seen that instead of the cream bond that might designate an invitation, there was instead a homely sheet of foolscap, which, save for the headline, *Horrida; Or, The Vampire's Bride*, was woefully blank.

A small crease appeared between the lady's eyebrows, and she absently nibbled on the tip of her plain wooden pen, at the same time emitting a small, frustrated sigh.

Somewhere between her majority and thirty summers, it could not be said that she was precisely a beauty, for statuesque, willowy females were much in vogue in that era of high-waisted dresses and flat-heeled shoes; her figure, while not heavy, was certainly given to curves, and she only stood a little over five feet in those ivory striped slippers. Then too, dark females were all the rage, and she was decidedly strawberry blond, as well as inclined toward the peachier end of a peaches-and-cream complexion, as was betrayed by the two bright spots of color that had begun to appear in her cheeks. But there was no denying the appeal of her regular features and heart-shaped face even as she frowned in a decidedly frustrated manner, tapping the nib of the now dry pen on the paper before her.

The teal eyes narrowed slightly and she thrust the workman's pen back into the incongruously elaborate Italian inkstand on the desk.

It had begun to occur to Miss Augusta Webb that for the past fortnight she had been staring, in anticipation of an apparently holidaying muse, at that precise piece of paper without so much as a word rising to her mind.

The dreadful suspicion began to dawn upon her that she was inflicted with that nemesis of all those who earn their living with the prose of their words. In short, Augusta Webb had writer's block.

With an exclamation of disgust, Miss Webb suddenly balled up the offending piece of foolscap and tossed it, with remarkable accuracy born of long practice, into the wastebasket.

"Brimstone and hellfire," she said succinctly, crossing her arms over her breast.

Perhaps fortunately, at that very moment there was the sound of the door to the morning room unlatching, and a very handsome young man, whose features proclaimed to the world his blood relationship with the lady at the desk, thrust his face through the door.

"I say, Goose, I know it's declaring war to

bother you when you're working, but I really *must* ask you—"

Augusta Webb turned about in her chair and regarded her brother William, late of the Fourth Dragoons. If he was expecting—and it might not have been unreasonable—an ink-stand hurled at his head for his breech of house rules, he was relieved to be greeted with a smile, however woebegone, and an invitation to enter at once.

"Oh, Billy! Thank God it's you! Come in here at once and talk to me." His sister, a decade older than himself, had never quite lost the idea that Billy was her baby brother, even though he was currently on furlough from one of the best regiments in Wellington's army and had been mentioned favorably in many dispatches before taking a ball in his leg and being sent back to England on a repairing lease that winter. "The most dreadful thing has happened."

Limping slightly, Major Webb crossed the room and seated himself with seeming carelessness upon the sofa before the hearth. Only the slight grimace that passed over his features betrayed the discomfort that still afflicted him from his wound, but Augusta, not unusually anxious over the state of her youngest and most beloved sibling, would have automatically bustled about with sympathy and cushions had she not understood Billy's pride and his extreme dislike of undue attentions now that he was past the dangerous stages of his wound and once again able to get about without assistance of a cane or a bath chair.

Pain had set a new maturity upon his face in the long and anxious winter of his convalescence, but there was still evidence of a boyish humor in the way he regarded his sister as he selected an orange from the bowl at his side and began to peel it with long, steady fingers. "I hope, Goose, it is not too terrible, for I had a late night, and my head feels as if all the blue devils of hell were dancing a jig in it."

"I heard you come in last night, it must have been almost dawn," Augusta started to say reprovingly and then, wisely, canceled her lecture in favor of a recitation of her own, more pressing problems, which, being Augusta, she did not hesitate to state in the most melodramatic terms.

"We are ruined," she announced, wringing her hands.

The major's right eyebrow shot up and he popped a section of orange into his mouth. "What, did your man of business run off with your royalties?" he asked lightly.

Augusta shook her head. "Worse," she said. "Writer's block."

If she was expecting a horrified reaction, she had mistaken her man. The major was not of a literary turn of mind, confining his reading to dispatches from Spain and the *Racing Form*, and was prone to regard his sister's unique avocation as something of a lark. Admittedly, it was a most lucrative lark, but a lark nonetheless. "What is a writer's block? Is it like a mounting block?" he asked.

"Worse and worse," Augusta sighed. "It means that I cannot write at all."

The major frowned slightly, turning this over in his mind. It might be said, even by so partial a judge as his sister, that while he was a veritable Adonis of a male, his intelligence was severely undisciplined, although in this manner hc was not too different from many of their friends and acquaintances in the upper ten thousand. Indeed, Billy was of a far more profound sensibility than most, when not afflicted with a severe case of the blue devils.

"What it means, you great booby, is that I cannot write," Augusta continued. "And if I cannot write, I cannot publish my new novel. And if I cannot publish my new novel, I shall have no advance. And if I have no advance, I shall have no royalties. And if I have no royalties, I shall have no money. I shall be dependent upon the capital that Papa left to you and there will be no more pretty little town house in Half Moon Street, and no more fashionable life in London, and no more Mrs. Parrot to run it all for us, and we shall be reduced to living in furnished rooms in Clapham Common, or very likely, I shall have to become a governess—and I shall not be comfortable at all!"

The major listened to this recitation with widening eyes, the fruit lying in his hand, dripping juice upon the Axminster rug beneath his feet. "Well, I don't think things can be all that bad," he finally managed to say, although there was some doubt in his tone, for Billy was not of a nature to give much concern to financial matters. "I've got my inheritance, after all, and my half-pay, and next autumn I shall be back with my regiment and on full pay again . . . well, dash it all, Goose, you needn't look at if you're staring down the bailiffs at the door, which there aren't, because Crockett would have told me if there were, no doubt Mrs. Parrot would turn them all to stone with one of her looks." A happier thought occurred to him. "Anyway, you've got a pack of great damned fashionable admirers dangling after you every afternoon, ought to marry one of them and have done with this scribbling about haunted castles and monkish specters. Sir Simon Swithin, he's got plenty of brass. Marry him, and all your troubles are over."

Augusta gave her brother a bald look. "Those haunted castles and monkish specters, as you so intelligently put it, have managed to put bread and butter on the table any time these past years since Papa stuck his spoon in the wall, and paid quite handsomely, also!"

"All right, then, your fashionable gothics!" The major conceded. "And yes, you have done all right with them, I will admit. Made you famous and rich and fashionable, which is not bad for a general's daughter from Somerset, I will admit, too. But hang it, Goose, just because you're having a little trouble coming up with a new plot doesn't mean you have to live like a nip cheese. There's always someone like Sir Simon lolling about, looking at you as if you was some kind of woodland sylph, which you ain't—"

"Sir Simon, you'd know if you had any sense, vastly prefers the company of his young male friends to mine, and anyway, if I'd had a chance to marry for love and didn't take it, why should I marry for money at this late date in my career? Do be serious, Billy."

"Maybe if you was to try one of those reducing diets, like your friend Byron—"

Augusta flapped her hands. "Oh, be still! That is not the point right now. The point is that Messieurs Clock and Fishbridge are expecting the completed manuscript of *Horrida* in a month, and I haven't even written the first sentence."

"Maybe all that horror and haunting has finally gone to your head, Goose. When you first started writing those things, I thought it dashed odd, 'cause you ain't morbid, and never have been, although you do enact a Cheltenham tragedy every now and then, but—"

"I thought I heard you both in here," said a well-articulated voice, and brother and sister glanced up to see a middle-aged female of forbidding mien standing in the threshold. A chatelaine depended from the waist of her sober gray round dress, and a plain linen cap covered her iron-gray hair, while ice-blue eyes studied them through forbidding steel-rimmed spectacles. To all outward appearances, this formidable female would seem more like to inspire terror than affection, but her erstwhile pupils both greeted her with loud claims for their side of the argument.

"Parry, if you would only listen to the great stuff and nonsense that Goose is tossing about, you would certainly laugh," the major exclaimed, inviting her to join his side.

"Parry, we are ruined," Augusta wailed to her former preceptress, throwing up her hands beseechingly. "I have writer's block!"

"William, you know that no one in the household is to disturb Augusta between the hours of nine and one," Mrs. Parrot said sternly to the major.

"Well, she invited me in," the major said, a trifle sulkily, thrusting his hands into his pockets and chewing the last of the orange furiously.

"Parry!" Augusta wailed again.

Mrs. Parrot shook her head and with a measured tread entered the room and seated herself in a chair opposite the sofa. "I am afraid I do not perfectly understand, Augusta. Pray tell me what writer's block might be."

"Obviously, my dear Parry, Goose can't write, and she thinks because she can't come up with a sentence or two, that we're all doomed to live in furnished rooms in Clapham Common."

Mrs. Parrot's lips settled into a line. Although no hint of it might have been apprehended by an outsider, she was quite as fond of her former pupils as they were of her, and still very much concerned with their welfare.

"As you will recall, my dears, before Augusta was able to publish her first novel, I was a resident of furnished rooms in Bath. It was no such mean fate as you might believe. However, I doubt very much that we shall be ruined if you should cease to write, my dear Augusta. In addition to what you have earned by your pen, your late papa left you an adequate competence—"

"Two hundred a year! Nip-cheese income!" Augusta sighed.

"There are many persons, you know, who would be more than satisfied to live upon two hundred a year," Mrs. Parrot reproved gently.

Augusta, who paid Mrs. Parrot somewhat less than that to run her household and provide her with companionship, had the grace to blush.

"And we have my six hundred, plus my half-pay," the major put in.

"Very likely, we do, but, my dear William, there will doubtless come a time when you shall want to marry and become the father of a family, and we must think of that."

"More likely we should think of what you

lost at cards last night," Augusta put in a little
pettishly. "Ever since you were able to leave
your bed, Billy, you've been out and about and
up to no good!"

"Here, now, a man's got to be up to every
rig and row in town," the major insisted. "I'm
no green'un anymore, if you're thinking of
that Captain Sharp who bulloxed me last
boxing day—" He grasped his head in his
hands, moaning in pain. "Blue-deviled,
William?" Mrs. Parrott asked sympathetically. "I know just the thing—castor oil and a
raw egg."

The major looked decidedly green as he
shook his head. "No, I thank you! I'll suffer
along with Burns' Headache Powders. The
point, Parry, is that Goose can't write."

Diverted from thoughts of castor oil and
raw eggs, Mrs. Parrot put her mind back to
the problem at hand. "It is hardly to be
wondered at, you know," she said calmly.
"Ever since the day that *Nightmare Castle*
appeared upon the bookseller's shelves six—
has it been six or seven?—years ago, and
forced Messieurs Clock and Fishbridge into a
second, then a third printing, and we
suddenly became fashionable and moved to
Half Moon Street—as you will recall, my
loves, we did—it would not be wondered if
after four novels, your muse has not deserted
you. After all, it would seem to me that of late
you have hardly found time to write at all.
Only take yesterday as my case in point. In the

morning you received a call from Lady Jersey,
who of course cannot be turned away, since
she was so kind as to procure you Almack's
vouchers when you first came to town. In
the afternoon, there was luncheon with
Messieurs Clock and Fishbridge, who were
most particularly anxious for you to meet
with the Regent's librarian."

"A very pompous gentleman, I might add,
who wore white gloves and informed me that
I was free to dedicate my next novel to the
Regent! *If* there ever is a next novel, which I
doubt!"

"If you please, Augusta, I am not finished,"
Mrs. Parrot said, holding up a finger. "After
lunch, you sat for Mr. Lawrence, and then
went with him and Mrs. Siddons to the Royal
Academy to view his portrait of Princess
Lieven, and in the evening, you gave a dinner
party for ten of your closest friends and then
attended a ball at Mrs. Hyde-Parker's—"

"And a dreadful nip-cheese affair it was,
too! Only one tray of lobster patties for a
hundred people, no champagne, and only one
orchestra," Augusta said petulantly.

"You seemed to be enjoying yourself hugely
last night," the major put in mildly. "You
never sat out a dance!"

Augusta bit her lower lip. "I do sound out-
of-reason cross, don't I?" she asked, "I shall
try to be better." She smiled weakly.

"And then, this morning, while you were
supposed to be closeted in the morning room,

working, you received morning calls from—"

"I know, I know!" Augusta threw up her hands. "But you know that no one may refuse to see Lord Byron—at least none of his friends, and I must count myself among that minority, if only because he is a fellow writer and we must needs stick together."

"Or hang separately," the major suggested rather evilly, reaching for another piece of fruit.

"Billy, you are unfair, and you know nothing about the matter," Augusta exclaimed. "Anyway, none of it signifies at all! If I could write, I wouldn't have gone *anywhere*! I'd be too exhausted."

"Precisely my point," Mrs. Parrot said equably. "If you will allow yourself due reflection, my dear Augusta, you will see that you are not writing because you lack the time. In short, you might be too much of a success."

"By far too fashionable is what Parry means," the major interjected. "You've come to London to see the lions, Goose, and you've become one of them."

Augusta propped her chin in her hand and looked from Mrs. Parrot to Major Webb, one eyebrow slightly raised in a weary cynicism. "All very well for you," she said, "but if I had not found an ability, however modest, to spin the most bloodcurdling ghost stories into novels when Papa died, where—"

"And very handsome novels at that," the major interrupted, "coming as they do from

Clock and Fishbridge, handsomely bound in three volumes, marbleboard at three and six and quite knocking the Minerva Press into flinders. My dear sister, your artistic temperament is flaring up."

His sister gave him a quelling look, but her sense of humor, never too far from the surface, began to bubble up, and she burst into laughter. "You are quite right! I do sound like the veriest harpie, Billy. Precisely like Lady Fortuna in *The Darkened Dungeon*, and she was one of my least favorite characters, because no matter what happened, she must needs whine and complain about it and fall into a swoon at the least sight of a ghoulish apparition or a spectral knight."

"You must admit, my dear Augusta, she held down the plot," Mrs. Parrot pointed out. "But I am forced to admit that I was less than fond of her as a heroine."

"And to judge by my royalty statements on that one, so was my public," Augusta observed. "However, it don't signify now, because the point is that if I don't think of some sort of story to drape about *Horrida*, much less a heroine, there won't be any new novel at all, and we can't have that."

"Furnished rooms," the major groaned in mock horror. "If you had been on our Spanish campaign, a furnished room in Clapham would have looked good to you."

"The sheerest bliss, I am certain," Augusta murmured absently, having spent her winter regaled with tales of smoky billets and hard ground.

"I think," Mrs. Parrot said at last, "that what is called for is a change of scene."

"An excellent scheme," the major exclaimed at once. "The Belles of Brighton, perhaps, or the Beauties of Bath? Town's dashed thin of female company these days."

Mrs. Parrot shook her head. "No, I was thinking more of a spell of rustication, away from the jaunt-about pressures of friends and acquaintances."

"The country?" Augusta asked, utterly horrified.

"The country," Mrs. Parrot agreed. "So peaceful, so quiet, so given over to the pleasures of pastoral simplicity. Fresh milk and vegetables, sweeping vistas—"

"Cocks that crow at daybreak and surly farmers reeking of manure? No, I thank you! I spent the first eighteen years of my life in the country, and never was I so glad of anything as I was to come to London."

"Ah, but, my dear, when you lived at Niepert, you had all the time in the world to devote to your writing, you know. Now that you are successful—and we are of course very grateful that you are so—it would seem that you no longer have the time necessary to devote to the long uninterrupted hours of peace and quiet reflection so necessary to a writer's life."

"You are on the town a lot," the major

pointed out. "Why, one may meet you any-where, Goose."

"I thank you, coming from my own brother," Augusta said sarcastically, "and considering some of the low haunts to which you repair."

"Precisely," Mrs. Parrot interjected meaningfully, and both ladies turned to study the major.

"Well, I say, a man who's used to a bit of action can't be expected to dawddle about Almack's every night," the major said defensively.

"Well, I am not the only person who could benefit by a change to country air," Augusta said meaningfully. "And now that I think about it, it seems to me that you should not be racketing all about the metropolis with a musket ball in your leg, brother dear."

"Country air, so bracing, so salubrious for you both," Mrs. Parrot said.

"Oh, no, oh no you don't!" the major exclaimed, much horrified. "If you think I'm going back to Niepert and bury myself in Somerset, you're entirely wrong, thank you very much! Grown quite accustomed to being a cliff-dweller! You two can book yourselves into the Hart and Hound or the Three Apples or whatever, but I shall stay here."

"Did I say a word about Niepert?" Mrs. Parrot asked mildly. "Heaven forfend. While I am certain that your brother Sir Wilfred and his good Lady Webb are everything that is genteel and amiable, I hardly think—"

"Now you are doing it brown, even for you, Parry. If you think for one moment Wilfred and Mariah want us to come and stay with them—and that pack of monsters they call children—for one moment more than we want to stay with them . . ." Augusta laughed, shaking her head. "Well, it won't do, that's all. Mariah's morbid piety and Wilfred's nip-cheese ways—"

"What Goose wants to say is that Mariah never forgave her for the portrait to the life that she drew of her sister-in-law in *The Specter of Lyndhurst*," the major interjected. "Brighton! Now there's something more like. None of your dashed slowtops there."

"No, I fear not! But as your sister's *dame de compagnie*, it is my duty to assure that she keeps only the most respectable company, and I hardly feel that Brighton has a reputation for being proper," Mrs. Parrot said repressively, with a sniff. "Some quite ineligible persons may be met there, and unless one wants to offend a very important personage, I fear one must acknowledge them."

"I think what Parry means," Augusta said, her eyes sparkling as she turned to her brother, "is that Brighton is full of the Prince Regent's mistresses—past, present, and future—and she has no wish for me to join their ranks."

"Why not?" the major retorted with a broad

wink. "Only look at what Lady Coyningham has gained from the alliance. They say she's been sporting a diamond the size of a dinner plate lately—"

"That will be quite enough of that," Mrs. Parrot said tersely, pressing her lips firmly together.

"If you mean to spare my tender sensibilities, Parry, have done," Augusta said baldly. "I may still be a spinster, but thanks to you, I have never been missish, and it has been a decade since I was in the schoolroom."

"Be that as it may," Mrs. Parrot stated firmly, "Brighton is out of the question."

"Forfend Bath, I beg of you, if I am to be included in this expedition," Major Webb cried, throwing up his hands defensively. "Assemblies that end at eleven, and all the old tabbies minding our business for us, no, I thank you!"

"Then it must be Scarborough for the Yorkshire heiresses!" Augusta laughed. "You must needs bail us all out of the River Tick, Billy, and set yourself up with some chit whose income outweighs her charms."

Her brother looked stricken at the very thought of marriage, but was quick enough with his rejoinder. "Well, if you had but pressed your suit with Mr. Muckleby and all of his ten thousand a year, then we should not be in our present fix, Goose."

"We are in no fix at all. In fact, we are at present quite warm, if I may say so," Mrs.

Parrot said, although she frowned at the idea of Mr. Muckleby. It has been her experience that gentlemen did not appreciate blue-stocking females quite as much as they ought, especially one as pert as her dear Augusta. There had been a very dashing young officer back in Somerset, but his expectations were not high, and the general had nipped that one in the bud, pinning his hopes upon the rather stolid Mr. Muckleby (and his ten thousand a year). Alas, Mr. Muckleby had disgraced himself and the village of Niepert by eloping to the Americas with the blacksmith's daughter, and Miss Webb had gone on to become a novelist. So, while it might have been Mrs. Parrot's secret dream to see her former charge bestowed well in matrimony, no suitor had since appeared who would spark her heart. And Mrs. Parrot was far too shrewd to advise her former pupil to marry where there was no affection; however much she personally might secretly repine that such a blooming rose was unplucked, she knew that Augusta could be lead, but not driven. For someone who wrote such thoroughly romantic tales, Augusta herself was singularly and almost repressively level-headed as far as the opposite sex was concerned. Perhaps the dashing young officer in that Somerset garrison town had burned her wings more badly than even Mrs. Parrot knew.

"I was thinking," she said aloud, her calm

tone betraying none of her thoughts, "more in terms of the seaside."

"The seaside?" Augusta asked, startled. "Pounding surf to keep you awake all night and the smell of fish—"

"The Hawkhurst gang," the major said somewhat obscurely, his eyes lighting up with sudden interest. "You know, smugglers and all of that."

"Not since Waterloo," Augusta said dismissively. It was the sort of thing she could be depended upon to know.

"The Sussex coast," Mrs. Parrot said, undaunted. "Sea air, so healthful, so invigorating. Fresh fish, so nourishing for a recent invalid, who was, if you will recall, at death's door only a few months ago. While I do not claim to be a physician, I would, if I were, prescribe a regiment of salubricity for both of you. A spell of rustication would do both of you a great deal of good."

At that moment, Crockett opened the door. "Lord Byron and Mr. Ruskin, miss. I put them in the yellow salon," he announced.

"Saved by the bell—or should I say the baron," Augusta exclaimed, throwing down her pen and rising from her chair. "Any excuse is a good one not to write, but Byron is always so full of the latest on-dits—"

She hurried from the room, leaving the major to study his apple core and Mrs. Parrot to glance heavenward.

* * *

The offices of Clock and Fishbridge, Publishers and Purveyors of the Written Word, were located on Milk Street, convenient to both the printing plants and the Fleet Street Prison for Debtors. Although Mr. Clock enjoyed his proximity to the former, he could never glance out his window without a shudder at the shadow of the latter, looming just over the rooftops.

A thin, skeletal man who seemed perpetually chilly, even in the balmy spring air that wafted through his open window, Mr. Clock worried a great deal about such things as going into debt, failing in business, and being placed in the Fleet. That was a part of his nature.

Mr. Fishbridge, his partner, was as round and rosy as Mr. Clock was thin and sallow, perhaps in consequence of the view from his window, which included the spires of St. Paul's. If Mr. Fishbridge worried about anything, it was not apparent, even to the thin and awkward clerk who thrust his head into his employer's offices to announce that Miss Webb and Mrs. Parrot had arrived.

Messieurs Clock and Fishbridge had been pondering the merits of a manuscript sub-mitted by a hopeful young poet, but at the mention of the arrival, however unannounced and unexpected, of their premiere authoress, the hopes of the poet were carelessly tossed aside and the good sherry produced from its hiding place in the cupboard.

"Show them in, Kent, by all means," Mr. Fishbridge said to the lanky clerk.

"Trouble," Mr. Clock predicted. "Authors only call upon us when they want an advance or to make an excuse."

"Now, now, Clock! Don't go borrowing trouble," Mr. Fishbridge advised, but said no more, for that was the moment that the lanky clerk, with an awkward bow, showed Miss Webb and Mrs. Parrot into the inner sanctum.

For this visit to her publishers, Augusta had toned down her appearance considerably. In place of one of her fashionable hats, she had chosen a drab bonnet with only a single ribbon cockade, and her pelisse was a last year's model from one of the lesser modistes, in a very dark blue with only a very small amount of silver braid. Her countenance was set into a grave expression, and the hand she offered in turn to Messieurs Clock and Fishbridge was limp enough to be almost lifeless.

"Money," Mr. Clock murmured under his breath to Mr. Fishbridge.

"Dear Miss Webb, and Mrs. Parrot, too. How well you are both looking, dear ladies," Mr. Fishbridge said jovially, lifting a pile of galleys from a chair in order to offer it to Mrs. Parrot. He tossed them carelessly on his already littered desk and escorted Miss Webb to his own chair.

"Sherry, ladies?" Mr. Clock asked. "So restoring in this changeable weather."

"Yes, please," Augusta said, in spite of the look she fetched from Mrs. Parrot.

As she accepted the glass, Augusta fondly looked about the cluttered offices, papered in such an ancient design as to be almost faded beyond recognition. It seemed to her that almost every available space was taken up with bookshelves, and still the volumes overflowed onto the floor, the desks, the windowsills, and the floor. And not just the books published by Clock and Fishbridge, but also the books from rival publishers, in particular, the Minerva Press. It could not be said that Clock and Fishbridge were about to allow the opposition to gain upon them; they were most interested in all the doings of their competitors and were not above luring away their more successful authors with promises of more money and better terms, both to be found at Clock and Fishbridge.

Clock and Fishbridge were hovering attentively about their premiere authoress at this very moment.

"Are you quite warm enough?" Mr. Clock was asking solicitously.

"Would you care for a macaroon?" Mr. Fishbridge asked, poised upon his toes to go out, if need be, himself, and find this favored delicacy.

Augusta shook her head. "No, thank you, I am fine . . . Well, I am not fine at all—that is the point!" She sighed and glanced at Mrs. Parrot, hoping for support from that quarter.

But Mrs. Parrot, sherry glass in hand, appeared to find the view of the Fleet utterly fascinating, and said nothing.

Augusta looked from Mr. Clock to Mr. Fishbridge. She swallowed hard. "Writer's block," she said finally.

If she had produced one of Wyngate's rockets from her reticule and proceeded to light it then and there in their offices, their reactions could not have been more horrified. Mr. Fishbridge's face lost a great deal of its rosy color, and Mr. Clock was forced to fold his thin body into a straightback chair. He picked up a long galley sheet from his desk and began to fan himself with it, opening and closing his thin lips as if in prayer to some deity of publishing.

Augusta felt worse than ever and twisted her hands in her lap. "You see, I won't be able to deliver *Horrida* on time because I haven't even been able to start it. I sit and I sit and I sit at the desk, every single day—"

"Except, of course, Sunday," Mrs. Parrot put in.

"Except, of course, Sunday, yes," Augusta agreed, watching Mr. Fishbridge's cheeks puff in and out with a terrible fascination, thinking he looked exactly like a bellows. "But every other day, you see, I do sit there. And nothing ever happens!"

"Nothing ever happens," repeated Mr. Clock, pulling out his watch and looking at it, as if he could count the overdue days, months and weeks upon its bland surface. "And we've scheduled *Horrida* for the printers in a fortnight."

"I'm sorry, but I don't know what to do," Augusta stammered, feeling very guilty indeed. "I've really tried, you know, but nothing happens. It's as if my mind is a complete blank."

"A complete blank," Mr. Fishbridge repeated. From an interior pocket, he withdrew a large white linen handkerchief and began to wipt at his brow. "Writer's block. Oh, dear, oh, dear, oh!"

Mr. Clock poured himself a second sherry and tossed it off. Then he poured himself a third.

Mr. Fishbridge took the decanter from him and helped himself. Evidently, the sherry fortified him, for he stood up and crossed the room toward Miss Webb, clasping her hands into his own. "Dear, dear, *dear* lady," he said, kneeling his considerable bulk at her feet like a suitor. "You must know how much Mr. Clock and I value your talents, your abilities, indeed, your genius—"

"Most positive genius," Mr. Clock put in, looming over the kneeling Mr. Fishbridge like a broomstick over a hay rick. "Oh, yes, value you. Our best authoress."

"If it's more money you want, only have your man of business contact us," Mr. Fishbridge said.

"Are you not feeling well?" Mr. Clock asked solicitously.

At the mention of money, Augusta looked rather bright, but Mrs. Parrot coughed repressively from her corner, and Augusta shook her head. "No, it's not money, and I am perfectly well, thank you. I simply cannot write."

"Cannot write," Mr. Clock said, wrapping his thin arms about himself and shivering. "Miss Webb cannot write, Mr. Fishbridge."

"But, my dear Miss Webb, you have written seven—or is it eight?—highly successful novels for us," Mr. Fishbridge protested. "You are our best authoress. We have only to announce that you have a new novel on the market and your readers virtually break our doors down in order to procure it."

"Three volumes, bound in marbleboard at three and six," Mr. Clock added. "Handsomely bound, I might add."

"Considering what Shoreditch and Ludlow charge us, they ought to be handsomely bound," Mr. Fishbridge put in. "But that don't signify to Miss Webb—or does it? You're not happy with the bindings? Only say the word and they shall be changed! Leather? Gold leavings? Tracery?"

Augusta shook her head. "No, no, all of that is more than wonderful. Indeed, no one could ask for better publishers than you have been for me, gentlemen."

"Then you're not going to the Minerva Press?" This dreadful thought seized Mr. Fishbridge, and he was forced to remove his spectacles to wipe them with his hankerchief.

Augusta pressed her lips together, lest she

betray herself with her smile. "No, I would never go to the Minerva Press," she promised them earnestly. "I simply can't write. I sit down with all the intentions in the world of doing so, and nothing happens."

Mr. Clock pressed his hands together in a dry, rubbing motion, and Mr. Fishbridge looked distressed. "Nothing happens."

"Have you tried cold baths?" Mr. Clock suggested.

"Have you tried a glass of wine?" Mr. Fishbridge asked.

Augusta shook her head. "Gentlemen, I have tried everything I can think of, but it's simply no good. I'm hopefully blocked."

"Physics!"

"Flirtations!"

"Music!"

"Utter silence!"

"A holiday!"

Messieurs Clock and Fishbridge looked at each other. Mr. Clock actually chuckled in delight. Mr. Fishbridge slapped his partner on the back and blew his nose.

"Of course! It always worked for Mr. Audley, didn't it?" Mr. Clock said.

"Invariably," Mr. Fishbridge agreed.

"What worked for Mr. Audley?" Augusta demanded to know.

"Holidays, of course. You recall Mr. Audley, the poet?" Mr. Fishbridge asked, wreathed in smiles of relief.

"What, that very old man-milliner who

write all those odes to postboys and pages?"

Mr. Clock dismissed this with a wave of his hand. "They sold very well, Miss Webb. Yes, every time he was blocked, he took a holiday."

"With a postboy, no doubt," Augusta said sharply. "I don't want to take a holiday. I haven't got the time."

"But it worked wonders for poor Audley, you know," Mr. Fishbridge said. "He always came back with reams and reams of verse."

"Where did he go?" Augusta wanted to know.

"Various places. The Cotswolds, Wales, Ireland. Wherever his fancy took him."

"Of course, it was too bad, at the end," Mr. Clock sighed.

Suspicious, Augusta looked from one to the other. "Why? What happened?" she asked.

"He took a holiday in Scotland and fell off a craig," Mr. Clock sighed regretfully. "But it don't signify," he added quickly. "I doubt if you'd like Scotland anyway."

"No, I don't think so. I don't think I want to go anywhere," Miss Webb said. "I hate the country. I grew up in a garrison town in Somerset, and the day I left there for London, I swore I would never, ever go back to the country again."

"But look what it did for poor Audley, Miss Webb. He produced volumes and volumes of verse, known by heart to every housemaid."

"Precisely so," Augusta exclaimed.

But before she could protest further, Mr.

Fishbridge was on his feet and Mr. Clock was summoning the lanky clerk.

"Kent," he commanded, "go 'round to the letting agents and see what they have in the way of country properties to let on a short term, the usual, just as we used to do with Mr. Audley."

"But—" Augusta protested.

"Now, now, Miss Webb," Mr. Fishbridge exclaimed jovially, patting her shoulder in a very paternal fashion, "don't you worry. Clock and Fishbridge can stand the pain. Nothing's too good for our best authoress, is it, now, Mrs. Parrot? Surely you must agree that a little rustication is precisely what our Miss Webb needs to work on *Horrida*?"

"Precisely, Mr. Fishbridge," Mrs. Parrot agreed complacently.

Augusta threw her a furious look, but Mrs. Parrot's expression remained bland.

In far less time than Augusta would have liked, Kent was back again, slightly out of breath as he scratched on the door and thrust himself and a portfolio through the opening. "Mr. Lundell's compliments, sirs, and he is particularly anxious for you to see the prospectus on a seaside property in Sussex, to let for six months at six hundred guineas, located directly on the coast, magnificent sea views, Tudor period, renovated, five bedrooms, three acres, beach ideal for sea bathing in season, all produce from garden and fruit from trees included in the let, part of an estate called Seaview, and Mr. Luddell says to tell you it's a whopping good bargain off the season." Kent swallowed and took a deep breath. "Also, Mr. Aintree's outside waiting to see you, Mr. Clock, about his manuscript on walking tours of the Outer Isles, and he's been there for an hour."

"Then he may sit there for another hour," Mr. Clock said. "Miss Webb's books outsell his fifty to one, after all. Give him some sherry and a macaroon."

"But not the best sherry," Mr. Fishbridge added, relieving the clerk of the letting agent's portfolio.

Kent nodded, his long neck sinking into his high cravat, and disappeared into the outer offices again, where, before he closed the door behind him, several interested clerks could be seen craning their necks from their high stools into the inner-sanctum offices. A visit from the fashionable Miss Webb was always a cause for curiosity among the lesser orders of Clock and Fishbridge.

"Walking tours of the Outer Isles indeed. Last year, it was the Cheviots," Mr. Fishbridge muttered as he adjusted his spectacles and opened the letting agent's portfolio. "Well, we have a cottage in the Cotswolds—"

"Rising damp," Augusta said, shaking her head.

"A fully furnished castle in Ireland," Mr. Clock noted, and immediately wished he had not when he saw the price of a year's let.

"Too far away," Augusta pronounced, much to his relief.

"A town house on Laura Place in Bath—"

"No, thank you. No Bath, ever!"

"A Queen Anne in Wales—"

"I am *not* the Ladies of Llangollen."

"Dear me, of course not, Miss Webb. Never suggested—and here is our Seaview Cottage, which comes highly recommended by Mr. Lundell, yes. 'Attractively situated property with magnificent vistas of the seaside . . . near Sea Cross, convenient to Rye . . . lovely little town, Rye, most picturesque . . . ' "

· "And the price, Fishbridge," murmured Mr. Clock, "is certainly right."

"If you please," Mrs. Parrot said suddenly, and the prospectus was passed to her. For several moments she studied it, a small twist of the lips, which may almost have been considered a smile in a lesser being, playing across her features. "And the owner, I see, is Baroness Towson," she remarked.

Mr. Fishbridge again removed his glasses and polished them on a handkerchief. "I wonder if she would be the widow of the late Lord Towson, the one who was such a great friend to the Prince Regent."

"To whom I will not dedicate a book," Augusta put in stubbornly.

"But, my dear Miss Webb, you have no choice. Royal command and all of that," Mr. Clock said, very much shocked. "Anyway, I would guess that having Lady Towson as your landlady would bode very well. An older female is hardly likely to take time away from your writing. Sea air, so inspiring, so salubrious."

"Oh, indeed, quite, quite healthy. Sea bathing and all of that. Beautiful vistas, plenty of healthy country food, blessed quietude. Perhaps the perfect place to write *Horrida*."

"But my house in London . . . Indeed, there are a hundred reasons why I cannot just pack up and go to the seaside—"

"We will take a few members of the staff with us and place the rest on half-wages," Mrs. Parrot said complacently.

"But—" Augusta struggled for reasons why she could not possibly allow herself to be whisked away at the height of the Season to some godforsaken cottage on the Sussex coast.

"Your contract states, Miss Webb, that if you do not deliver us the completed manuscript of *Horrida*, in fair copy, you must return your advance," Mr. Clock reminded her, putting on the screws in his best editorial manner.

"Dear, dear Miss Webb, we have your best interests at heart. We want to see you happy and productive." Mr. Fishbridge beamed. "Sea air, so conducive to the muses . . ."

"But—"

"We'll be glad to accept your kind offer,"

Mrs. Parrot said, handing the prospectus back to Mr. Fishbridge. "And I am certain that Miss Webb is very, very grateful for all of your kind attentions to her, aren't you, dear?"

When Augusta could close her mouth, she did so, but it took her several seconds to reply. "Oh, yes," she said, with only the faintest trace of sarcasm in her voice. "Most grateful!"

Messieurs Clock and Fishbridge beamed. "Then it's all settled," they said in unison.

2

The wind had been sullen all day. Now that night was falling, it began to pick up a little at first, and then quite a bit, carrying the air of the sea on its currents.

As the heavy traveling coach rolled over the rutted and pocked post road, Major William Webb dropped the flap and thrust his head out the window, inhaling the sharp tangy wind deeply. "I say, you can smell the sea on the air—we must be quite close," he announced to his two companions within.

Mrs. Parrot looked up from the traveling chessboard on the cushion between herself and Miss Webb, her spectacles glittering. "We are fortunate in that we have the advantage of a full moon," she remarked, "else we might have lain tonight at Tunbridge Wells. Check, my dear Augusta."

But Miss Webb was not listening, for, like her brother, she had broken the latch and was twisted into a most unladylike position against the squabs, disarranging her elegant little chip-straw toque as she leaned out into the black and silver night. "I can smell the sea," she exclaimed. "You're right, Billy. Oh, it cannot be too far now."

"Very likely not," Mrs. Parrot said, exerting a firm hand upon Miss Webb's feather tippet in order to induce her to return to a more decorous position on her seat. "But you will recall, if you please, that ladies do not hang out of carriage windows."

"By Jove, no, Goose," the major exclaimed. "Surely you recall that Banbury tale about the little boy who leaned out of the carriage window and had his head severed by the Dover mail."

"Fustian," Miss Webb called back, peering into the darkness as if she hoped to see the Channel over the next rise and hillock, but when such was not the case, she resettled into her seat, smoothing down the skirt of her merino pelisse as if nothing had happened. "We just passed the road sign for Sea Cross, so I daresay it cannot be too far now," she added. "Oh, Parry, you beast! Checked!"

Mrs. Parrot allowed herself a tiny smile. "If you would apply yourself to the game rather than deploying yourself by handing the windows, you might have seen my queen coming for your knight," she said.

In his corner opposite, the major thrust out his long legs with a painful grimace and suppressed a yawn of fatigue. "Only hope," he said a bit sulkily, for he was often slightly out of sorts when overtired, "that this is all worth it, Parry. I could have been at Boodle's tonight."

"And very likely in dreadful straits tomorrow," Augusta replied for her governess, sliding a chesspiece hesitantly across the board. "Well, it's too late now to pine for the Season; we've taken a half-year's lease upon Seaview Cottage and I daresay the baroness will be most upset with us if we were to renege on our agreement now."

"I only hope she's not the sort of old tabby who will check upon all our comings and goings and count the silver every time Crockett makes a move."

"I doubt it very much—if she's friend to Mrs. Oglesby, I have no doubt but what she's an ancient dowager. Very probably she goes about, when she does, in a bath chair, with a footman carrying her gout stool," Augusta conjectured, removing her fingers from her pawn, which Mrs. Parrot triumphantly captured with her handy queen. "Parry, you are unfair!"

"Only observant! Pray take note that one cannot play chess and converse at the same time, my dear," Mrs. Parrot said.

Augusta stretched a little. "Then I shall concede the game to you entirely, Parry. Dear, I wonder what we have fetched ourselves into this time. Six months by the sea, and at the height of the Season, at that! I only hope I shall find a spectral mermaid or a selchie in the bath—"

"Selchies live in Scotland, not Sussex," the major put in, thrusting his hands into his pockets. "Very likely you will find no supernatural horrors, but rather the horrors of provincial society, all of them ready to leap upon us like a wolf at the kill. Matchmaking mamas and rustic squires, dying to make up to the famous London authoress."

"No, I thank you. I do not mean to go into society, as we agreed. We shall keep our own company and depend upon the visits of our friends from London to make us less dull while I'm working. If we had wanted provincial society, we could have stayed at Niepert."

Major Webb shuddered eloquently. Restless, he shifted in his seat. "Star light, star bright, first star I see tonight, I wish I may, I wish I might, have the wish I make tonight," he recited carelessly, looking out the window. "I wish," he said more clearly, "for an adventure!"

Both women looked at him rather strangely. "I should hope that it was never said to me that I am superstitious," Mrs. Parrot said a trifle repressively, "but you must recall, William, the old adage that one must be careful what one wishes for, for one might receive it."

The major's lip twisted upward in the slightly cynical smile he had developed during his long convalescence. "Well, you must admit, an adventure would be just the thing. I'm not used to these slow top ways after Spain."

"I daresay after Spain we should all be glad of a little dullness," Augusta said somewhat sharply. "Certainly, its consequences were anything but dull, not knowing from day to day if you would live or perish of the fever—"

Billy flashed a grin at his sister and merely shrugged his shoulders. "Females," he said loftily, "can't be expected to understand."

"Very likely not," Mrs. Parrot interjected smoothly, thus putting an end to any further sibling bickering.

Later, the lumbering carriage was suddenly brought to a jerking halt. Outside, there was the sound of the coachman's oath and the braying of the team.

William, who had been drowsing in his corner awakened with a start, and his hand went to the small pistol tucked into the waistband of his buckskin trousers.

The chessboard had been thrown from the seat, and the pieces were scattered about the floor, rolling beneath the feet of the two ladies, and Augusta's toque was knocked askew. "Highwaymen?" she asked, a trifle wide-eyed.

"Very likely not," Mrs. Parrot said, unruffled. "William, drop the trap and see what is going on, if you please."

But before the major could implement this action, the door swung open, and in the dim light of the lantern, the three passengers blinked at the sight of a darkly handsome gentleman of a decidedly foreign aspect. Or at least Augusta, the most observant of the trio, would have identified him as not being English, for the cut of his elegant driving coat, as well as the elaborately waxed hussar moustaches that adorned his upper lip, was decidedly more Continental than English. When he spoke, his accent confirmed her suspicions instantly.

"A thousand pardons, *madame, mademoiselle, monsieur*," he said, exhaling a blast of fine old port into the already close space of the coach and sweeping his hat off to reveal a head of blue-black and intensely pomaded curls. "But, you see, with my phaeton I was attempting to pass your coach and I misjudged my distance." He hiccupped slightly and gripped the panel of the door for support, swaying slightly. "*D'accord*, my phaeton is now one wheel in the ditch, and my groom and your coachman and 'ostler are so kind as to extract it from the situation."

The major's hand did not relax its grip on the pistol concealed in his coat, and unconsciously his eye strayed toward Mrs. Parrot's expression, searching out her intuition. But her bland, somewhat forbidding countenance betrayed nothing of danger, while Augusta's betrayed a great deal of amusement.

The stranger smiled, revealing a flashing set of perfect white teeth. "So, you see, it is I

who have embarrassed you . . . or rather, it is
I who am embarrassed, and I mus' beg
your—hup!—pardon."

"Is anyone injured? The horses?" Mrs.
Parrot asked sensibly.

The foreign gentleman shook his glistening
curls. "My pride only, *madame,* and for that
I—hup!—offer a thousand pardons. I am . . .
comment dit-on? yes . . . a trifle foxed!"

"Indeed, sir, you are," the major said
testily. "Ought to let your groom take the
ribbons."

The foreign gentleman nodded. "Ought to!
Yes!" His bleary eyes surveyed the major
apologetically. *Mais, c'est dangereux,
comprenez-vous,* this mission." In his attempt
to look quite serious, he failed, and his
countenance took on the look of a woebegone
clown. "*Il faut* that *monsieur le comte et
madame la comtesse* be avenged, even if
vengeance takes fully twenty years." He
looked grimly from one face to the other.
"Yes, revenged," he insisted. "*On ne l'oublie
pas!*"

Augusta, who like all writers was most
insatiably curious about the business of
others, immediately looked interested. "I am
afraid that we do not perfectly understand
you, *monsieur,*" she said enticingly.

The foreign gentleman swayed a little as he
studied her face, but just as he was about to
open his mouth, a second man in the livery of
a groom appeared in the shadows and placed

a hand upon the gentleman's shoulder, speaking in a low and rapid French that none of the passengers in the coach could quite comprehend.

A drunkenly crafty look passed over the gentleman's face and he nodded to his groom, before giving the ladies a sweeping, if somewhat awkward bow. "Again, a thousand pardons. My man assures me all is well and there is no harm done to either vehicle. *Adieu, mesdames, monsieur.*"

Without another word the door was latched and the trap let up. The heavy coach lumbered into motion and Augusta sat back on the seat, looking rather balefully at her brother.

"There!" she said. "You see what comes of making wishes? You wished for an adventure and now we have had one that we shall never know the end of."

"And very probably just as well! What a deuced odd sort of fellow," the major said, peering out the window. "There he goes. By Jove, there's a phaeton and pair—perfectly matched bays, from what I can see. Well, the groom's driving him, so I doubt he'll kill anyone else tonight."

"One would sincerely hope not," Mrs. Parrot said, picking chess pieces out of her skirt. "It would be most inconvenient."

"Just feel fortunate that we are not in one of my novels, or that would have been an omen," Augusta remarked. "A wretchedly bad omen!"

3

Luckily Augusta did not believe, as did her fictional heroines, in omens and portents, for if the incident of the drunken foreigner did not put her off, then surely her first glimpse of Seaview should have sent her back to London in a great hurry.

Peering up at the darkened house, where not so much as one candle in any of the black, blank windows signaled a welcome to the travelers, Miss Webb stepped from the carriage and felt a definite sense of foreboding that was in no way relieved when the clouds scuttering across the rough and uncertain water parted to reveal the full face of the moon shining down upon Seaview Cottage.

"*This* is a charming seaside cottage?" she asked, incredulous. "Parry, it would appear more to be a seaside mausoleum."

As if offended by her comment, the overgrown ivy that covered the ancient walls of the structure stirred in a sudden gust of wind, casting long shadows along the darkened windows. Somewhere a loosened shutter banged hollowly, the only sound in the night save for the jingling of the weary horses' harness. Obviously of Tudor origin, it was apparent to Augusta that very little had been done to improve the house in the intervening two hundred years. A ramshackle affair, rambling without concern for symmetry or design over an ill-kempt-looking lot, it seemed to sit and brood over its new occupants with a forbidding aura, in no way decreased by the sharp overhang of its low rooflines and sheltered diamond-pane casements, winking in the moonlight as clouds raced across the moon. That it was surrounded, indeed, fenced in, by a planting of huge and ancient oaks effectively blocking off a great deal of its vaunted view of the sea (as well, Augusta had no doubt, as a great deal of daylight) somehow made it even more ominous and threatening.

"Oh, I say, Goose, it looks as if you created it," the major said, turning from paying off the coachman to have his first good look at the house. "It would appear as if no one were here either."

"In her letter, the baroness was very clear that there would be some help for us until Crockett and Polestack arrived," Mrs. Parrot said.

"Well, let us see if we can get them out here to move some of these trunks, or else we ought to turn back and lie at the inn in Sea Cross tonight," the major suggested.

For a moment, the three of them watched

the hired coachman beating a hasty retreat down the long lane, and a slight feeling of foreboding might have crossed all of their minds as the noise of the horses' hooves receded into the distance.

"Perhaps they have all despaired of us and retired for the evening," Mrs. Parrot suggested, stepping up to the heavy iron knocker in the thick old door. For a moment, it seemed to Augusta as if the lion's head with the iron ball clutched in its teeth might be winking hideously at Mrs. Parrot as she held it firmly in her hand and let it fall back against the door, but she quickly decided it was her imagination.

For several seconds, they stood listening to the hollow booming sound echoing deep within the bowels of the house, but there was no response, and Mrs. Parrot, in her best no-nonsense manner, sent forth a second volley, which rang out like artillery shot.

"That would wake up the dead, Parry," the major said, and laughed a little uneasily, shifting the weight off his lame foot as Augusta shivered in the dank air.

But the desired effect was secured, for from within they could hear the sound of bolts being drawn back and locks shot before the heavy old door creaked open an inch and a ghostly, unshaven face peered outward, muttering suspiciously.

"Good evening, my good man," Mrs. Parrot said imperiously. "The Webbs have arrived to take possession of the house."

"Don't know nothing about any Webbs," said a high, crackling voice, and had not Mrs. Parrot thrust her umbrella into the crevice between door and jamb, she would have found it slammed in her face.

"Not so fast, if you please! This is Miss and Major Webb, and they have leased Seaview Cottage from Lady Towson, so if you will be good enough to let us in ..." With an expert twist of her wrist, the umbrella defeated the last resistance and the door flew backward against the protests of the ancient within, who stood in the dim light of a tallow candle, his rheumy eyes peering over at Miss Parrot with great resentment.

"You'll have to go back, I say," he cried in his old man's voice, making shooing gestures with the candlestick as Mrs. Parrot calmly stepped back and beckoned the Webbs to enter. "Back, I say, back, back, back!"

He was certainly forbidding enough to Augusta, who took a step backward into her brother. Whether it was in fear of this sinister retainer, so typical of the stereotype with which her novels were loaded, or fear of tallow wax staining her traveling pelisse, was somewhat in doubt.

Augusta was quite certain she heard her brother swallow very hard, but Mrs. Parrot remained undaunted, peering at this apparition over her spectacle rims as if he were some not very appealing specimen of insect.

"I beg your pardon?" she asked in her most

frigid tones, drawing herself up to her full height, which, while not impressive in itself, taken together with her considerable girth was apt to make an impression, even upon a spectral domestic.

The ancient hesitated in his purpose, and was lost. "What I mean to say is, you're not due until tomorrow. No place for you to stay here. Have to go to the Bird and Feather in Sea Cross." To illustrate his point, he lifted his candle, affording them a view of what appeared to be a parlor, shrouded in holland covers and dust in equal parts.

"Gad," said the major quite succinctly, and sneezed.

"There!" the ancient said triumphantly. "You see? Not fit tonight! Come back tomorrow. That's when Lady Towson's sending a crew down from the hall! All will be ready for you then."

Mrs. Parrot sniffed in disapproval. "There can be no mistaking the date, my good man, it is the twenty-sixth, and we are here, as I informed Lady Towson we would be."

"Nay, nay, it is the twenty-fifth," the old man protested. "I've been with the Towsons man and boy for fifty years, and I know the twenty-fifth when I sees it, and you ain't here on the twenty-sixth."

"There can be no mistake. *I* do not make mistakes," Mrs. Parrot retorted, and showed him her pocket calendar.

Although Augusta was fairly certain that

the caretaker was illiterate, he made a great show of peering closely at the figures before grudgingly announcing, "Well, then, it must be as you say, ma'am, but how it came to be, I do not know. Eh, my lady, now, she's liable to get flitterheaded from time to time."

"Doubtless, she is senile," the major whispered unkindly to Augusta. "As senile as this one, no doubt."

Augusta gave her brother a repressive glance and was rewarded with an expression so angelic she was tempted to give him a very strong pinch.

Mrs. Parrot, tucking her calendar back in her reticule, said, "If you will rouse up someone to take our baggage up to our rooms, I think we might do with some tea and bread and butter before retiring."

The caretaker exposed toothless gums in what might have been meant as a chuckle. "Ale and a bit of 'prridge is all you're likely to get here, ma'am. I was engaged as a caretaker, not a cook." He closed one eye and regarded them all from the other. "And anyways," he wheezed, "surely you wouldn't be wanting to sleep here tonight—the beds ain't made, nor yet anything come out of covers, not till tomorrow when Mrs. Peavy do come down from t'hall with the girls. A-settin' of this place to rights is Mrs. Peavy's job, not mine. By rights, I ought to have retired. I only stay on here to oblige the late lord, y'know. It's what he would have wanted us to do, look after my lady . . . Now, surely, sir, you'd be much happier if you was to rest at the Bird and Feather, hey?"

Augusta glanced about uncertainly at the shrouded and dusty rooms, but Mrs. Parrot stood her ground. "Nonsense, my good man. You may very easily apprehend that the coach has departed, and you would hardly expect us to walk to Sea Cross at night. What cannot be fixed must be endured, and if you will be good enough to show us to the bedchambers, I daresay we shall contrive well enough on short shrift until things may be attended to by Lady Towson."

The old caretaker looked as if he had a great deal more to say upon the subject, but Mrs. Parrot fixed him with her eye and looked very much as if she meant to give him a sharp set-down, and he quavered, dropping his own gaze, knowing when he was defeated.

He only muttered as he shouldered their portmanteaus and bade them follow him up the carved Elizabethan staircase, where the light of the flickering tallow candle Mrs. Parrot had comandeered from him threw eerie shadows across the traceries in the wood.

"If there are not ghosts here, I should be very disappointed," the major said, grimacing a little with the effort of climbing the risers on his injured leg.

Augusta was pleased to note, however, that his eyes danced with mischief, and she only retorted, "Very likely we shall be haunted by rats and bats."

She had not meant her remark to be overheard, but the caretaker nodded vigorously, turning in midflight to look down at them.

"No," he said in a warning tone, "no vermin here! My lady wouldn't have it." A crafty look came into his expression and he grinned toothlessly, lowering his voice, "If you're afraid of ghosts, now . . . well, that's a different story entirely." He paused bringing the party up short. "In the old lord's salad days, his aunt lived here. Disappointed in love, she was, and withdrew here to brood about it. She grew quite barmy in later life, and swore she heard the ghostly hoofbeats of her dead lover coming up the drive after her on nights such as this."

Three pairs of eyes looked up at him, and sensing that he was holding his audience, he pushed onward. "Oh, aye, I was but a stableboy in those days, but I can recall her well: she paced about the cottage at all hours of the night and day, always wearing the same white dress, till it had fallen into tatters, her hair turning gray and standing up all over her poor head as she wrung her hands, over and over and over again calling for her poor lost lover. Sometimes as night falls and the storms brew off the water, I think I can still hear her calling . . . It's fair enough to give a man the frights, it is, that sound, like a shriek . . ."

"That, my good man, is quite enough of

that," Mrs. Parrot said abruptly. "I doubt very much if the spirits you see come from the beyond or from a bottle. Now, if you will be good enough to conduct us to our rooms, by tomorrow our own people shall have arrived, and you will doubtless be able to retire to your own cottage." She shook out her skirts, looking very much like the bird of her namesake, and fixed him with a sharp and beady look.

The old caretaker sighed and shrugged. "Well, now, you can't say that I didn't warn ye off," he said, slowly proceeding up the stairs. "If you're found dead in your beds upon the morning, with looks a fear on yer faces, it will not be my fault."

"Very likely," said Mrs. Parrot. "We shall relieve you of that responsibility, at least!"

On the upper landing, Mrs. Parrot discovered a candelabrum. With somewhat more illumination, she was able to assign rooms to herself and her two erstwhile charges without any further protests from the caretaker. This individual even went so far as to direct her to the linen closets when she complained that sheets laid down upon beds left unused for nearly a year must surely be unhealthily damp.

With very little energy left for the sort of jests that might have ordinarily been made, the party separated for the duration of the night, one last warning from the ancient caretaker ringing in their ears as he descended the back staircase to his own quarters.

"Just recall, in a storm, I can't hear ye screamin'," he delivered as a final good-night, and the sound of his muttering gradually faded.

Augusta, had she been given her choice, would have doubtless stayed awake all night, though not in fear of ghosts. In spite of her themes, she had no faith in the supernatural, but she did have a fear of those marauding rats emerging to nibble her toes. Also, she certainly would have liked to deliver her opinions of ill management and shoddy housekeeping and the leasing of houses by the sea to Mrs. Parrot, but upon finding herself alone with a heavily ornamented four-poster bed, all she could think about was lying down upon the mattress and going off into an exhausted sleep. It took all her strength to drag herself out of her clothes and into her nightdress before she was beneath the counterpane and off to sleep.

If an entire horde of ghosts decided to hold a three-ring Astley's show in the bedroom, she thought as she drifted off to sleep, she could not have cared less, so great was her fatigue.

But when, much against her will, her consciousness began to surface in the dead watches of the night, it was not the thought of ghosts but of rats that brought her up between a state of wakefulness and dreaming, for in her dreams, the soft, scratching sound

she thought she heard in the room seemed to
come from a merry parade of these small and
odious creatures trooping gaily across the
floor and up upon her bed. . . .

With a start and a muffled exclamation,
Augusta awakened, sitting bolt upright in the
bed, her hands seeking to sweep rats away
from the counterpane.

But they met only air, and she opened her
eyes to see a shadowy figure, silver in the
beam of moonlight that fell from the window,
caught in the act of tapping at the paneling on
the wall, and seeming quite as startled to see
her as she was to see it.

4

"What?" Augusta exclaimed somewhat incoherently, clutching her pillow protectively against her nightgown bodice.

The silvery figure froze for only an instant and then made a low and muffled sound that could easily have been something along the lines of "So sorry" before disappearing into the paneling.

Where he had gone—for she was certain, in the brief glimpse she had been afforded, that the figure was masculine—or what his purpose had been, she could not immediately determine, and it was several seconds before she could force her thundering heart to assume a more normal pace.

So swiftly had this episode passed that she was not entirely certain that it had occurred at all, but rather that it had been the product of a dream. She thought of removing herself from her warm bed to cross the cold floor and shiver as she attempted to investigate the possibility of this as a reality, and then thought better of it. The bed was too warm, the possibility of a bad dream too secure, and her mind entirely too prosaic to accept any other plausible explanation.

She burrowed herself back into the pillows, pulling the coverlets up over her head. "That," she murmured sleepily, "will teach me to listen to the demented ramblings of ancient retainers."

And so, chiding herself for her lack of common sense, she fell back to sleep.

When she awakened again, the sun was streaming in the windows, and a cock was crowing somewhere. As she lay abed, collecting her thoughts for the day, Augusta studied the room and found thtat it was by no means as unpleasant as her first impressions had led her to believe. True, it was paneled in a heavy and darkish oak, carved with grinning feral men and bunches of grapes, but with the sunlight streaming through the windows illuminating the grain of the wood, it almost seemed cheerful. There was an ancient clothespress, and a Charles I chaise covered with needlepoint cushions, and a high bureau beside a pier glass, all pieces of great age and the sort of luster that comes from centuries of use. A couple of Meissen bibelots stood upon the mantlepiece, and there was a framed watercolor of Rye hanging on the wall above the bed.

Augusta stretched, yawned, and pulled herself up from the great depths of the eiderdown mattress. She padded across the room and opened the diamond-pane casement, allowing the sea air to pour over her. Dropping her hands in her chin, she contemplated the view.

Down from the ivy-covered walls of the house to the terrace below, sunlight reflected a harmony of old stone and green vine. The lawn stretched down toward the sea, where it abruptly dropped a few feet to a tiny strip of sandy beach. Gentle as a kitten's tongue this morning, the waves lapped at the sand, and the blue water beckoned to the horizon. "France is just across the water," she said to herself, and thought about that for a moment. Born in a generation raised up in the isolation of the long wars with Bonaparte, she had never been to France, nor indeed anywhere on the Continent. It was somehow exciting to think that the coastline of a foreign shore lay just beyond the horizon, but it also, in some convoluted way, recalled her to their adventures of the night before, and she bit her lip, frowning at the ways in which imagination could run away with one.

There was a knock upon the door, and she turned just in time to see a thin, competent-looking woman in a plain black dress, carrying a tray, enter the room. "Good morning, miss. I trust you slept well? I am Mrs. Peavy, the housekeeper from the hall . . ." As she spoke, she placed the tray on the nightstand, removed the lid to reveal a full English breakfast, and dropped a curtsy. "Lady Towson sends her compliments and her apologies concerning the mixup, and hopes that you will not take too much offense if I direct the girls this morning in a thorough course of cleaning." Two bright spots flamed in the woman's cheeks and she shook her head. "If you don't mind my saying so, miss, her ladyship is likely to forget things—at her age, you see—"

"Oh, I am certain no offense was taken," Augusta hastened to reassure her, drawing on her dressing gown and gazing hungrily at the scrambled eggs and ham on the plate. "And I do understand. I'm certain that at Lady Towson's age there are a great many things one cannot quite recall."

Mrs. Peavy nodded. "So she sent me over as soon as Cooley came to tell her you were here, and ordered me to do my best to see all is made right before noon. I only hope Cooley didn't upset you too much, ma'am. He's old and set in his ways, and as like to be foxed as night by the time the sun's set down. It's just that there ain't too many of us anymore to look after her ladyship, and someone's got to stay on at the cottage to look after it, if you take my meaning."

Augusta, bidden to eat, had poured her coffee from a silver pot and was falling to with gusto when Mrs. Peavy uttered this last, and she looked up at the housekeeper questioningly. "I am afraid I do not," she said, shaking her head. "I am not from these parts, you know."

"Ah, well," Mrs. Peavy said cheerfully

enough, as if that explained it all. "Well, the gentlemen, you see . . ."

"The gentlemen?" Augusta asked blankly.

"Smugglers, miss. If the house weren't attended to, you may be certain that they'd know in a trice, and the next thing you would find was Inland Revenue peering into all of our storage houses looking for kegs and brandy and French silks."

Augusta's eyes danced. "Oh? My brother would be quite interested to know that. He was certain the country would be a dead bore."

Mrs. Peavy smiled. "The poor gentleman was knocked up this morning, I fear. The trip must have exhausted him, and him with a wounded leg on top of it all, poor thing!" She shook her head in a maternal way, and Augusta realized her brother had found a staunch supporter.

"Is Mrs. Parrot awake?" Augusta asked next, and the housekeeper nodded. "Oh, yes, we've had a nice cup of tea and I've taken her all over the house, showed her where things are, so that when your people arrive, they will know just how to contrive. She's a lady as knows how to hold house," the housekeeper added with respect. "I daresay she could teach my lady a thing or two."

This remark struck Augusta as extremely odd, but she said nothing at the time, for the breakfast Mrs. Peavy had brought her was delicious and required her full attention.

"Eggs fresh from the home farm, and the ham is from our own hogs," Mrs. Peavy pointed out proudly. "I daresay you'll note while you're here that everything tastes better in the country than it does in London."

"Indeed, and I thank you for bringing it to me," Augusta said gratefully.

"Well, it was the least we could do, after my lady's mistake," Mrs. Peavy said, shaking her head. "My lady is something of a flibberti-gibbet, but there, it can't be helped, so was the late lord, and they do say such things run in the blood, like red hair or blue eyes."

"Ah, there you are, Mrs. Peavy," the major exclaimed, bursting into the room without salutation. "Come and tell me at once about these ghosts of Cooley's, else I shall perish from curiosity!"

Mrs. Peavy shook her head, wiping her hands on her apron. "Now, Mister Billy, don't you go listening to that old man! He's always been a great bag of wind, and more than likely he was trying to afright you into going away so that my lady couldn't accuse him of not doing his job properly, which I can assure he has not. The dust I've seen downstairs is enough to make a body who takes pride in her housekeeping cry."

"But you will set it all aright, I have no doubt," the major said airily, snatching a piece of toast from Augusta's plate and consuming it with marmalade. "I need it more than you do, Goose! I'm a growing boy," he said with a wink to his sister. "But tell us, Mrs. Peavy, all about the haunted aunt, driven mad by love?"

Mrs. Peavy sighed, shaking her head. "There was no haunted aunt. True, a long ways back, when the old lord was but a boy, his great-aunt did live here, but she was as shrewd as could hold together, and the oddest thing *she* ever did was keep twenty-seven cats." Her expression became unreadable, and she continued slowly. "Oh, there are ghosts here, all right, ghosts at Seaview, but not the sort of flay boggerts who moan in the night and rattle chains. That would be simple enough to deal with, compared with the load of problems we have."

She stopped, and it was clear that she felt as if she had said too much, for she abruptly dropped a curtsy. "And now, if there's nothing else, I must see to the girls. They'll be laughing and chattering among themselves and not lifting a hand if there's no one there to tell them how to go on."

As soon as the door had closed behind her, brother and sister gave each other a puzzled look. "What do you suppose she meant by that?" Augusta asked.

The major lifted his shoulders. "Doubtless, we shall find out. All families have secrets, you know."

"Yes, and I suppose we shall find them all out, whether we wish to or not," Augusta replied thoughtfully. "Although I cannot see

anything particularly fascinating about an
aged and decrepit baroness."

"Well, Goose, you never know. She may
have a tragic history."

Augusta stood up and shook out her
dressing gown. "I daresay everyone about this
place has a tragic history," she sighed. "And
they will all be dying to tell me about it in
hopes that I shall put it in my book!"

Her morning was given over to a tour of the
house and grounds in company with Mrs.
Parrot, and she found them by no means as
forbidding as they had seemed upon the
previous night. The house was not quite
Elizabethan, but Jacobean, and the furnishings reflected an antique but comfortable
setting. With an small army of housemaids at
work until noon, it was not very long before
the old pieces gleamed again, offering a
warmth and comfort that far outweighed any
disadvantage of style.

"I think that we shall manage to be
tolerably comfortable here," Mrs. Parrot
pronounced, and Augusta did not disagree,
particularly when she had seen the
magnificent vistas to the sea offered from the
eastern windows.

Fortunately, all was in good order when the
second carriage bearing the rest of their
luggage and Crockett arrived, in company
with Miss Polestack, Augusta's taciturn
abigail, to set up housekeeping. Crockett pronounced himself very well satisfied with the
arrangement he reached with Mrs. Peavy in

that two of the maids from the hall would come down during the day to wait upon them and help serve at table, and he managed to produce a very tolerable luncheon for the three of them from the provisions he had brought down from London.

They were just rising from the table when the elderly butler appeared in the doorway of the dining room, bearing a card upon a silver salver.

"Lady Towson, miss. I have taken the liberty of placing her in the drawing room," he announced as Augusta removed the card from the tray and confirmed that their landlady was indeed their first visitor.

"Poor old thing!" Augusta said sympathetically. "We must go to her at once. I daresay it cost her a great deal to make it down here this afternoon."

"Cannot you make my excuses?" the major asked plaintively. "The groom has brought my horse down from London and there is nothing I would less like to do than spend an afternoon in the company of some old tabby, listening to gossip about people none of us knows."

"That would be quite improper," Mrs. Parrot said repressively, and the major heaved a long-suffering sigh as he trailed the ladies down the passageway.

"Very well, but don't say I didn't warn you if my leg starts to act up," he muttered sullenly.

Which was perhaps why no one was as

startled as he when Augusta opened the drawing-room door upon a petite young lady in a black merino pelisse, perched upon the sofa.

"How do you do?" she asked at once, rising to meet them and holding out a hand clothed in York tan. "I am excessively sorry about Cooley, but he has been with us forever, and one simply can't turn him out. I trust Mrs. Peavy has set everything to your satisfaction? I can't tell you how embarrassed I find myself! It is extremely mortifying to lease a house to *the* Augusta Webb and then mistake the arrival date."

Augusta took the hand that was offered to her, looking about the room for an aged and senile dowager in vain. "How do you do? I am Augusta Webb, and this is Mrs. Parrot, and my brother, Major Webb. But where is Lady Towson? Her card was sent into us—"

The girl laughed, and Augusta noted that she was very pretty, with masses of blue-black hair and ice-blue eyes framed by dark, long lashes, set in a flawlessly featured heart-shaped face. "Ah, but you see, *I* am Lady Towson," she announced, smoothing the bands on her wrists. "The late lord's daughter. One of those titles that descend in the female line, you see."

"Ah," the major said, and it was more like a sigh as he took the Yorktan-gloved hand held out to him. The blue eyes met his own for a single second, and two bright spots of color flushed into her cheeks before Lady Towson dropped her gaze for just a second.

"Pleased," she murmured.

"You will forgive me, but I was expecting a very old lady—a dowager," Augusta said, flustered.

"Not quite," Lady Towson pealed, diverted. "I am only nineteen, you see."

"Indeed," the major breathed, and Lady Towson's eyes fluttered to meet his gaze again.

"Oh, I am sorry," Augusta murmured.

"Will you please sit down, Lady Towson?" Mrs. Parrott interjected smoothly, and the lady delicately perched on a corner of the sofa before the fireplace, the major nudging his siter out of his way in his eagerness to be seated beside her.

"Thank you," the baroness said brightly, turning enormous eyes toward Augusta. "You are truly *the* Augusta Webb? The authoress of *Castle Gaunt* and all the other wonderful novels?"

"I am indeed," Augusta acknowledged gravely, only the faintest upturn at the corners of her lips acknowledging her amusement.

"There! I told him so, and he would not believe me," she exclaimed artlessly. "Only fancy, having someone like you here, where absolutely *nothing* ever happens. I have read all of your novels, Miss Webb, and loved them excessively, particularly *The Darkened*

Dungeon. That scene where Reynaldo climbs up the face of the cliff and rescues her is . . . well, I wish someone would climb up a cliff and rescue me, save, of course, there are no cliffs in this part of the country, but, oh, it was so romantic, you know, and the Loup-garou Abbe, so terrifying!"

The major looked very much as if he would have volunteered to climb a cliff, but perhaps happily, Lady Towson did not notice, for she prattled breathlessly onward. "Mrs. Mill-banke, at Anchor Hedge, you know, says that it is great shame that I stuff my head so full of romantic notions, but I ask you, what else is there to do in a place like this? Since Papa took his header and left me in charge, everything's been at sixes and sevens, and although I tried to love Papa, it is really vexing to me that the estate should stand in such bad condition as it does, and Mrs. Millbanke says that it is all on account of Papa marrying Mama, who escaped, you know, from the Terror in a basket of cabbages—she was only a baby, then; an adult couldn't hide in a basket of cabbages, could they? But Papa's excesses were a result of losing Mama, and of a course, Seaview has gone to rack and ruin, so we are obliged to let out the cottage—some relations of my mothers lived here, you know, after the Revolution and all that happened there. I am supposed to be remarkably like my mama, but since I can barely recall her, I don't have the faintest idea what she looked like—but my cousin, you know, says that Papa could have at least educated me to my station, rather than allowing me to run wild and stuff my head full of novels, but you write novels, for of course I have read them all, and he can certainly have no objection to you as you are of the utmost respectability—"

Lady Towson paused to draw a breath, and Augusta seized the opportunity to put a handkerchief to her lips, while Mrs. Parrot occupied her hands with her tatting work. Only the major continued to gaze at the little baroness as if he could not drag his eyes away from her.

"We are so cut off here, you see, quite out of the way. Papa went to London and to Brighton a great deal—he was a particular friend of the Prince Regent, you see, which is how he came to slip that fence and break his neck at Melton Mowbray. Tell me about London, if you please! Are paisley shawls like yours all the crack this winter? As soon as my mourning is over, my cousin—he is my guardian, you see—means to take me up to London and have me presented. I suppose I shall have to marry a fortune as I have none myself, only this estate, which, as you see, Papa was not at all attentive to, and which Robert—that is my cousin—says has been run into the ground without a groat being put back into it. But Papa was as fine a Roman parent as they say the Prince Regent is to poor Princess Charlotte."

Lady Towson paused again, and Augusta

judged her silence meant that she was awaiting a reply.

"Alas, I do not move in those circles," Miss Webb said gravely, "and therefore know nothing more of the matter than you."

"It is a great deal too bad, for I imagine that everyone here believes you to be the very first stare of fashion, which I do not think the Prince Regent is. He seems very old and very out of sorts to me, or at least he did the one time he came here to visit Papa, but it may have had to do with the fact that he was losing at cards that night, and probably gouty to boot. D'you think, when I go up to London, I might have a shawl like that?"

"Oh, no! Something far grander than just an old paisley shawl," the major said in a dreamy voice, looking at Lady Towson as if she were the moon and stars. "Something silvery and gossamer, like your laugh."

Lady Towson turned and looked at him, a smile creeping up her expression. "Thank you. You are very kind," she said.

Augusta, who had paid dearly for her shawl, could only stare at her brother staring at the baroness. Never in her life had she seen him act like this, and it began to dawn upon her that he was upon the verge of being besotted with love for the first time in his life. She exchanged a glance with Mrs. Parrot, who merely raised an eyebrow and continued with her tatting.

"How exciting it will be to have you here,"

the baroness said, looking directly at William. "I mean all of you," she added ingenuously. "You may be sure that your appearance in the neighborhood will be cause for excitement, and lots of parties. Doubtless they will not be as grand as those when the Regent was here, but it will be better than the assemblies in Rye and the little dances Mrs. Hunt gets up for her daughters. Imagine! Four daughters to launch! Not that I should talk, for I doubt any man will want to marry me when he discovers how badly mortgaged the estates are." She shook her head ruefully. "Of course, Robert, my trustee, is a complete hand at management. But still, one wishes one had a guardian who were not quite so strict. I suppose it was all right for him when I was at school, but there really was no reason for Mrs. Oglesby to keep me on in Bath when I was of an age to come out, and besides, it was only a very little accident with firecrackers, and nothing at all improper."

Augusta's glance again flew to Mrs. Parrot, but that lady merely made a sympathetic sigh as she continued on her fringe, so there was no enlightenment to be found there.

"Robert is almost as Roman as my papa. He will not let me dance the waltz, or stand up for more than two dances with one boy in Rye, at the assemblies, and he has the most odd notions of female propriety! He—"

At that moment, the door of the drawing room opened, and a gentleman stepped into the room. Clearly he had been out riding, for he wore high top boots and a buff-colored hacking jacket and held a high-crowned beaver in his hand, but other than appearing before them unannounced, there was nothing in his person that should have made Augusta first gasp and then start in her chair the moment he spoke.

"Forgive me for coming in upon you unannounced and in all my dirt, but her groom told me that Lydia had ridden over this way—I am Lydia's guardian, Robert—"

"Robert Darnley!" Augusta gasped.

5

For what seemed to both parties to be forever, Robert Darnley and Augusta Webb stared at each other across the room.

Her face was drained of all color, while his had turned a peculiarly ruddy hue, and a muscle in the side of his jaw worked itself in agitation. He stood frozen in the doorway for several seconds, the knuckles of the hand that gripped the riding crop turning white.

For her part, Augusta had started in her chair, and the hands that clutched the carved wooden arms of her seat were shaking. Her eyes were as large as saucers, and slowly, two bright spots of color flamed in her cheeks, made brighter by the whiteness of her complexion.

"You," she said in tones utterly devoid of expression.

"Yes, it is I," he replied evenly enough, although his eyes were wary.

To the interested eyes of Lydia and William, there was nothing in Robert Darnley's appearance that should have caused Miss Webb such consternation. He was a tall man, well formed, but without any eccentricity of appearance that would have made him in any way remarkable. Indeed, there was a certain attractive quality to his countenance, with its heavy brow and heavier eyebrows overshadowing a pair of penetrating dark eyes. Both his nose and his jaw were strong, but leavened by a humorous set to his lips and a slightly quizzical expression about the eyes. His dark hair curled generously about his face, softening the harshness of its lines considerably, although in moments of agitation, such as this, he was likely to thrust a hand through those curls, disarranging them considerably.

"I must say, I hardly expected to see you again," were his first words to Miss Webb, after he had recovered himself somewhat.

"Nor did I expect to see *you*," she retorted, sinking back into her chair.

"I take it you two know each other?" Lydia asked, her eyes darting from one to the other with a lively curiosity.

"Oh, yes," Augusta said without taking her eyes from Robert Darnley's face. "We were friends—once."

He looked as if he wished to say something, but Mrs. Parrot, whose iron composure was never ruffled, laid aside her tatting and offered a hand to the visitor. "How do you do, Colonel Darnley?" she asked. "It has been nearly a decade since we last chanced to meet, at Niepert Garrison."

Taking his cue from her sangfroid with some relief, Darnley smiled as he bent to take the hand she held out. "Mrs. Parrot! You seem to be doing well. It's Mr. Darnley now, though—I sold out long ago. Although, of course, I should always want to be Robert to you."

Augusta threw Mrs. Parrot a furious look. Had it been up to her, she would have had Crockett show Mr. Darnley the door then and there. But when she was able to speak again, her voice was much more level. "I hardly expected to meet you here—or, indeed, *anywhere*, sir!"

"Nor I you," Darnley replied evenly. "Particularly considering the circumstances of our last meeting."

Augusta flushed up to the roots of her hairline.

"So, you two do know each other," Lydia exclaimed. "Were you once sweethearts? How very romantic!"

"I think a little less of your runaway tongue might serve you well, Lydia," Mr. Darnley said heavily, frowning at his ward.

"There!" Lydia said triumphantly. "You see how he treats me! It is all quite gothic, and I appeal to you, Miss Webb and Mrs. Parrot!"

Mr. Darnley looked at Lady Towson in such a way as to imply he would have liked to deliver her a strong set-down, but Mrs. Parrot stepped smoothly into the breech.

"Mr. Darnley, I do not believe that you have met Major Webb, Augusta's brother. When you were stationed at Niepert Garrison, the major was still at school."

Gravely, Darnley shook hands with Billy. "So, you're the fellow Wellington spoke so highly of in his dispatches from Waterloo?" he asked. "The Eighty-ninth?"

In spite of himself, the major flushed with pleasure. "The Fourth The Bravo Boys. It wasn't just me, you know! Stroke of luck—and bad luck." He hit his leg to illustrate.

"Stroke of genius is more like," Mr. Darnley said warmly. "I tried to reenlist when Boney escaped from Elba, but it was all over before we could cross the Channel. So, you are General Webb's son? You have his look about you, you know."

"You served under my father at Niepert Garrison? You must have been in Spain, then."

"Only for a short time. But that was nothing compared to the Bravo Boys. Your father would have been proud of you."

"I would like to think so, sir," William said shyly. "He always had a high regard for Old Hook, you know."

"Yes, I knew General Webb quite well. I was his A.D.C. for a time at Niepert." He looked as if he might like to say more, but instead pressed his lips together and stole a glance at Augusta.

For her part, Augusta was studying him with interest. It had been more than a decade since she had last set eyes on him, on his wicked lying face, and she was somewhat disappointed to see that no evidence of his betrayal had eroded his strong features, nor in any way did he look like the dissipated monster she had devoutly hoped he would become over the years. True, he was aged a little. There was gray in his dark curls, and the lines that ran between his nostrils and the outer corners of his lips were deepened, but she was dismayed to note that she still found him as attractive as she had when they had first met at a garrison dance in the war years. Was this the callous young officer who had broken her heart? How odious he was, acting as if she had been the one who had jilted him! Of course, Papa had not approved of him at all, and had done his best to pull them apart, but still, if Robert had really loved her, one might have thought that . . .

"I trust your prospects have brightened considerably in the past decade? You seem to have prospered," Darnley said to Augusta, changing the subject.

"Oh, indeed," Augusta said coolly. "I am odiously fashionable now. You may see me—or any one of my novels—almost anywhere."

William, who was unused to his sister being anything but modest about her accomplishments, gave her a strong look, which Augusta ignored, laughing a little unsteadily as she added, "Oh, yes I have come 'all the crack!' "

"There," Lydia said naively. "I told you she was fashionable, did I not, cousin?"

A vague look of contempt flickered behind Mr. Darnley's smile. "Miss Webb has long desired to be attended to, and I am pleased to note that she is aware of her own value as a celebrity. However, I think it would be best if you did not attempt to emulate her, ah, self-confidence, Lydia. It is not becoming in a young lady."

"So you always say, cousin, whenever I say the least little thing that strikes you as improper," she retorted, a little heatedly.

"How long have you been Lady Towson's guardian, Mr. Darnley?" Mrs. Parrot inquired in an attempt to steer the conversation into more general topics.

"Six months, but it seems more like a year," Mr. Darnley said with a hint of exasperation in his voice. "I am my lady's only living relation, I fear," he added ruefully.

"And you cannot wait to be rid of me, either," Lady Towson said, bristling slightly.

"No more than you can wait to be rid of me, brat," Mr. Darnley replied with a grin. "I may say to all here that I never expected to have the charge of a schoolroom miss placed upon me at this late stage of my life, any more than Lady Towson expected to have me foist off upon her as guardian."

"Exactly so!"

"Exactly so," Mr. Darnley repeated dryly, rising to his feet. "And now, my lady, I think it best if we were to go back to the hall and allow these folks a chance to settle into their new house, do you not think so?''

It was apparent by the look on Lydia's face that she did not, in fact, think so, but she only sighed a little as she rose and very prettily made her good-byes to the ladies.

''Do you ride, Major Webb?'' she asked as he took her hand.

''Oh, yes,'' the major said, enraptured.

''Then we shall have to ride. If you will come up to the hall at teatime, we will go around to view the stables.''

''That would be above all things capital,'' William promised, as if he had gone to heaven on the promise.

''Absolutely, do come—it will be good to have some male company, and we may talk about the military without boring the ladies to death,'' Mr. Darnley enjoined him before making a very civil bow to Miss Webb and Mrs. Parrot.

They were no sooner gone than Augusta rose from her chair and began to pace the room. Mrs. Parrot, apparently quite unruffled, resumed her tatting, ignoring the smoldering glances Augusta threw her from time to time.

''That man! Of all the places on this green earth that he should turn up, to think that it would be here,'' she exclaimed in terms of utter loathing. ''And to think that he could sit here, in my drawing room, and talk to me as if nothing had ever passed between us!"

"Now, now, my dear Augusta," Mrs. Parrot said, tatting away as if she were not listening at all.

"Only to think the way he made me suffer and suffer and suffer, waiting all those long terrible hours, cramped in that terrible little room with a bandbox, thinking he would come and we would be off to Gretna Green, when instead he was aboard a troop ship headed for the Continent! Oh, I could savage him yet. Odious, pompous, conceited wretch!"

"I think you judge Mr. Darnley too harshly, my dear," Mrs. Parrot said absently. "After all, it was your father who ordered his transfer—it was not precisely his own doing, as I have told you many times."

"Yes, but he could have stood up to Papa," Augusta fumed. "Imagine! Oh, Parry, do you recall how blue-deviled I was for months and months afterward?"

"Of course I do, my love, and then your papa died and you had other things on your mind."

"Oh, yes, I did! And all that time, I waited for a letter from him, and never did I receive as much as a line. Not even a message. Heartless, callous wretch!"

"Oh, I have always depended a great deal upon Mr. Darnley's character," Mrs. Parrot said complacently. "He was never heartless."

"Great wretch!" Augusta repeated

stubbornly. She looked at Mrs. Parrot with dawning suspicion in her eyes. "My dearest Parry, surely you did not *know*—" she began.

If ever Mrs. Parrot could have been said to smile, it might have have been at that moment that a flicker appeared at the corners of her lips. "Mrs. Oglesby is a great gossip," she said, tatting on.

"Parry, that is impossible! You cannot expect, after all these years, that I would possibly ever entertain—or that Darnley would ever entertain any notion of—"

"You must admit, my love," Mrs. Parrot said complacently, snipping a loose thread with her little scissors, "that he has aged quite handsomely."

Augusta threw up her hands. "Impossible! He could be the veriest Adonis and I would not be moved. Never, never, never!"

"*Never* is a word that we do not use," Mrs. Parrot said in her governess voice.

At that moment, William limped back into the room again, his face aglow. All of the fatigue and tiredness of his illness had been erased from his features, and he was wreathed in beatific smiles. "Oh, I say, isn't she the most wonderful, the most ravishing, the most thrilling of all creatures?" he asked dreamily.

"Who?" Augusta asked blankly, her mind entirely upon the many reasons why she would forever deny Robert Darnley entrance to Seaview Cottage.

"Lydia," William said, "Lydia. Even her name is music. And to think that as I helped her up on her horse, she smiled and pressed my hand and thanked me."

Augusta exchanged a look with Mrs. Parrot. William was clearly in the throes of a long-delayed first love.

"Well," Augusta said as she flounced out of the room, "I only believe that he is more than enough punished with having that hoyden in his charge. Let that serve upon his plate as his punishment."

"Whatever is Goose talking about?" the major asked.

Augusta decided it would be entirely within Mrs. Parrot's province to straighten the matter out and left to seek some privacy.

As she walked into her own room, she saw that there would be no solace or privacy, for Polestack, her abigail, a grim-faced female of undetermined age, was busily sorting out her trunks in a welter of tissue paper and ribbands.

Before Augusta had a chance to speak, Miss Polestack held an object up between thumb and forefinger, as if afraid it might bite.

"And what," she inquired gruffly, "are we to make of this, Miss Webb? It *was* among your things."

Augusta stared at the decidedly masculine leather writing case Miss Polestack was displaying for her edification.

6

It took several moments for Miss Webb to focus her attention upon the offending object, for her thoughts were quite naturally occupied with her recent interview with Mr. Darnley to the exclusion of all else. Indifferently, she shrugged, seating herself at the dressing table, where her fingers mindlessly played over the combs and brushes Miss Polestack had laid out upon the old wooden tray. "I daresay it belongs to Mister William," she said absently.

Miss Polestack, a thin and withered female of an indeterminate age, shook her head, watching her mistress's face in the mirror. "Varney disclaims it belongs to Mr. William," she said. "And I found it among your portmanteaus, so it must have come up with you in the post coach, miss."

Augusta was absently pulling the pins from her hair, barely conscious of her own actions, and she merely nodded without interest.

Polestack, who had been with Miss Webb since she first put up her hair and let down her skirts to appear in society, studied her employer for a moment, her expression unreadable, before she placed the writing case on a chair and crossed the room, picking up a hairbrush and beginning to brush out the tangles in Augusta's strawberry-blond hair.

Although Miss Polestack had not the faintest idea what had caused her mistress's upset, she knew that having her hair brushed out always soothed Augusta, and she applied herself to this task with a professional demeanor that well concealed her interest in events below. Since she was reasonably certain that Miss Webb's distress was caused by the inordinate disorder of the let house, she clucked her tongue sympathetically and allowed as how the staff would be very well-settled very soon, with things just as Miss Webb liked them.

When this elicited only a faint smile, she continued to brush with long, soothing strokes until she felt the tension dissolving in Miss Webb's neck, and more as a diversion than anything else remarked, "The reason we were so delayed, miss—and I'm sure Crockett should have told you, if he did not—was that there was a terrible accident on the road, just outside Sea Cross. It would seem that a drunken gentleman was driving one of those nasty, dangerous high-perch phaetons down the road last night, being more in his cups than he should have been, and he managed to overturn himself and all his team in the darkness, running right across the road and into a ditch. Well, they didn't find him until this morning, and his groom dead of a broken neck, and all his horses having to be put down for one cause or another, and the phaeton mangled all out of shape. We come upon it all, with the men trying to pull the phaeton out with a team of oxen, and the dead horses all lyin' in the road, and it was something horrible, miss, to see," Polestack said with all the relish of one who enjoys morbid tragedies of others. "Well, the poor gentleman, although he had no business to be so foxed and out upon the road, was just barely alive, they did tell us, and had been taken to the doctor's house in Sea Cross, where he lies right now, if he's not lying out on the trestle, which he very well might be. They said he was some sort of foreigner seen before in these parts, although no one knew his mission."

In the artless prattle, Augusta's mind suddenly seized upon something, and she turned around, dragging a lock of her hair through the brush Miss Polestack held in her hand. "A foreigner?" she asked, suddenly interested. "Perhaps a Frenchman?"

Polestack pressed her lips together, gently disengaging Miss Webb's hair from the bristles of the brush. "Well, miss, I'm sure I couldn't say, for they had long borne him off when we came upon the scene—and a right nasty scene it was, too, all blood and screaming horses and the groom lying there under someone's coat, but you could tell his neck was broke from the angle—"

"Then that must be his writing case," Augusta exclaimed, starting up from the chair and picking up the leather case.

"I don't see how—" Polestack began, but Augusta was already attempting to open the lock.

"It would tell us, of course, something inside would," she said, guilty of a writer's curiosity, if nothing else, "if we could only open it, but we can't because it's locked." She shook the case hopefully, but it made no sound, whatever it contained being tightly packed inside.

Quickly, she explained the events of the previous evening to her puzzled maid, who merely pursed her lips in disapproval, being strongly Chapel and Temperance. "Well, miss, no good can come of it now. Two accidents in one night, and all because of drink! Well, I doubt very much, from what we heard this morning of his condition, that he shall ever have need of it again, nor any other mortal thing on this earth."

Augusta sighed and placed the writing case in her wardrobe. "Well, I daresay we can investigate it all later, unless you would hand me one of those hairpins—perhaps I would prise the lock and then we could discover what his mysterious errand might have been. Very odd events in a place where I daresay nothing ever happens."

"Very odd indeed, miss, and no, I would not allow you to try to prise it open with a hairpin! Whatever would Mrs. Parrot say?"

Augusta, having lost interest and returned to her brooding concerning Mr. Darnley, merely shrugged indifferently, seating herself before the dressing table again and signaling Polestack to recommence her ministrations. "I shall ask her later today, when there is a free minute," she said. "Doubtless she shall know the answer."

Her intentions, however, were displaced when Crockett knocked upon the door and announced that Mrs. Parrot had sent him upstairs to fetch her down, since there were lady visitors in the morning room.

"A Mrs. Leigh and a Mrs. Hunt, Miss Augusta," he said, his eyebrows twitching expressive of his opinion of provincial society.

When Augusta entered the morning room again, she was as reasonably composed as Mrs. Parrot might have wished, and no one could have detected from her coolly polite demeanor that she had suffered one of the great shocks of her life only a few hours before.

She found Mrs. Parrot seated calmly upon the striped sofa, while a very large lady and a very small one, having appropriated the set of flanking chairs, seemed to be glowering at each other in a fashion Augusta found most unneighborly.

"Ah, there you are," Mrs. Parrot said, and only those who knew her very well indeed could tell there was a faint trace of relief in her voice. "May I present to you our neighbors, Mrs. Leigh, of the Grange, and Mrs. Hunt, of the Larches. Ladies, Miss Webb."

Both ladies flashed broad smiles upon her, while managing to frown at each other. "So pleased to meet you," they both said at once, and again daggers were shot in looks across the room.

Seating herself beside Mrs. Parrot, Augusta declared herself very pleased to meet them.

"It is not often that our neighborhood is honored by the presence of an authoress," Mrs. Leigh began. She was, indeed, a very large and matronly woman, attired in a dress trimmed in a great deal of lace, while the hat that sat upon her grizzled curls featured a bit of, it seemed to Augusta everything: fur, feathers, a diamond clip, a large bow, and several bunches of artificial flowers. The entire effect was very startling, for so much ornament could not help but emphasize her avoirdupois, which was considerable.

"Indeed, my dear Georgianna, exactly what *I* was about to say, had not I been interrupted," Mrs. Hunt said in icy tones. She was as tall and thin as her neighbor was short and heavy, her boniness emphasized by the dark severity of her brown bombazine dress and the stark black turban she wore over her suspiciously dark, flat hair.

"I'm certain you were, my dear Henrietta," Mrs. Leigh pronounced in deadly tones before flashing her enormous, consuming smile at Miss Webb and Mrs. Parrot. "I am such an admirer of yours, Miss Webb. I think that I have read every book of yours save *Glencavern*, which mysteriously disappeared from the lending library right after Mrs. Hunt borrowed it." Again, she shot a look across the room at her neighbor, whose sunken cheeks caved in indignantly before she replied.

"I'm sure I could not comment upon that. I have always been most precise in returning volumes I have borrowed, unlike some people in these parts." Her smile, directed toward Augusta, was that of a grinning skull. "*I*, Miss Webb, am not only a great admirer of your work, but also an admirer of all things literary, although you can, of course, have no idea of the philistinism of what passes for society in these parts."

"T-thank you, both of you," Augusta said a little unsteadily.

"Of course, my dear Miss Webb, it is unfortunate that you will encounter a great many mushrooms in our little area," Mrs. Leigh said, tracing the design in one lace mitt with the fat finger of her other hand, "persons of somewhat dubious gentility who will attempt to present themselves as cultured to you. But I am certain that you will only be interested in the very best families and the very best entertainments while you are staying in our little neighborhood—"

"Which is why, of course, I called this morning," Mrs. Hunt put in quickly, leaning forward in her chair, her long, bony fingers clutching at Augusta's skirts. "I wanted to invite you to a little soiree I am getting up on the twenty-first, quite an intellectual set of persons—"

"Oh, my dear Henrietta, I am certain that Miss Webb and Mrs. Parrot do not want to be sucked into one of your little evenings at the Larches on the same evening when I will be getting up one of my little country dances—"

"Only, my dear Georgianna, if they like stale cakes and watching a group of society children attempting to dance the waltz," Mrs. Hunt retorted meaningfully.

Augusta blinked, putting a hand to her mouth to conceal her laughter. "I am certain that both of your proposals have equal merit," she said.

"Oh, we have become quite gay in these parts with so many new and interesting people," Mrs. Leigh promised. "Mr. Darnley and Lady Towson, dear Lydia, such an unfortunate event for her—"

"Unfortunate!" Mrs. Hunt sniffed. "Lucky is what I'd call it, lucky that the late lord didn't run her inheritance any farther into the ground than he did, and so I'll tell the world."

"I doubt very very much that anyone would care to ask you, my dear," Mrs. Leigh said coolly, turning her attention back to Augusta. "But I hope that you will not find us dull here. We may not be London, but we do manage to be gay."

For several moments, both ladies rambled on, between attacks on each other, begging her to grace a variety of entertainments that Augusta began to feel very strongly were being created simply for these two rival hostesses to find an opportunity to place the literary lioness on view. Nonetheless, Mrs. Parrot graciously accepted for all of them, and there was very little Augusta could do but try not to fidget in her seat as the two ladies challenged each other with proposals for country dances and counterproposals for little suppers of not more than forty persons of the very best sort, routs, musical evenings, card parties, or drums. To all of this Augusta listened uneasily and with the growing certainty that she should be compelled to encounter Mr. Darnley wherever she went, whether she wished to or no.

Throughout all of this chatter between Mrs. Leigh and Mrs. Hunt, Augusta tried to keep a pleasant smile on her face, but inwardly she felt as if she were being crushed. Even as her common sense was telling her that she had nothing to fear—or feel—about Robert Darnley any longer, she still felt a twinge of the old heartache whenever she considered standing up with him at a dance, or catching a glimpse of him across a roomful of strangers.

Too, how long would it take before the entire neighborhood discovered their painful history? Certainly Lydia would have teased Robert until she discovered something, and knowing Lydia, it would be only a matter of time before she shared her knowledge with the world at large.

And that would be unbearable. . . .

"I was saying, Miss Webb, that it is a great deal too bad that Alfred de Hasard has returned to the Continent," Mrs. Leigh repeated a little loudly, and with a start, Augusta was brought back to the conversation at hand.

"Alfred de Hasard?" Augusta repeated blankly.

The plumes in Mrs. Leigh's hat nodded vigorously. "Then you do not know the previous occupant of the cottage?" she asked. "I thought he was everywhere received in London!"

"Which only goes to show how little you know of tonnish events, Georgianna." Mrs. Hunt smiled a thin smile as she stroked her tippet. "Alfred was not at all an intellectual."

Mrs. Leigh drew herself up to her full height in her chair. If she had feathers, they would have ruffled. "I beg to differ with you, Henrietta, Alfred was *quite* intelligent."

Mrs. Hunt smirked. "But that is totally different from being literary, my dear," she purred. "But it doesn't signify, save to persons of a very low order. He is a delightful young man, so polished, so charming. We all miss him since he returned to France to claim his family's estates."

"A most romantic story, you know. How one does miss him!" Mrs. Leigh sighed. "He was always one to make everything so much more amusing. He was a most-sought-after guest, dear boy."

"His manners were so very nice, and his taste . . . Well, my dear, when the de Hasards lived here at the cottage, it was the brightest I have ever seen it."

"Not a feather to fly with, of course; they lost everything they had in that dreadful Revolution. I understand that they were smuggled out of Paris under a load of cabbages or something equally dreadful."

"Of course, the older de Hasards never got over it—the shock, of course. It was what killed the old gentleman, they say."

"And she died soon after, and there was Alfred, you see, with very little. Oh, they'd managed to get some jewels and such out with him, but if it hadn't been for Lady Towson—Lydia's poor mama, one always finds it so hard to remember that little Lydia is now Lady Towson, after all, so strange, don't you think, when titles are passed in the female line—Debrett is quite right, it does mangle everything up so, and what will they call her husband, I wonder?"

"I believe, Georgianna, we were discussing poor Anne-Marie."

"Oh, yes, poor Anne-Marie. She was French, you know. Towson met her on a trip to Paris. They had to marry, you know, although not for that reason, although it seems to me that Lydia did arrive amazingly soon thereafter, but of course, it was the religious question."

"In the end, she converted to C. of E., so that was all right, but when the Revolution came, with all those nasty beheadings or whatever, poor Anne-Marie was already dead, and Towson running wild. He was not a nice man," Henrietta sniffed. "A friend of the Regent's, you know. Let Seaview go to rack and ruin. A terrible thing."

"So, of course, when the de Hasards suddenly appeared—they were Anne-Marie's cousins, you know—he put them into Seaview Cottage."

"Not a word of English among them. All French, French, French. The old lady and the old gentleman never did get their tongues around our language, but Alfred adapted amazingly well."

"Of course, I daresay Mr. Darnley was glad enough to see him go. I for one, am very fond of Mr. Darnley, but he just could not stand dear Alfred. Thought him frivolous, I suppose. But then Towson never liked Alfred either."

"Nor did he like Mr. Darnley. But Mr. Darnley was his first cousin, you see. Mr.

Darnley's mother was Lord Towson's younger sister, before she married and moved to Hampshire, so of course he had to name Darnley as his trustee."

"Poor man, too! What a mess Towson has left him to straighten out—a proper tangle! It's a good thing the estate's entailed, or Lydia would have precious little to call her own save that title."

There was some tongue-clucking here, and both ladies shook their heads sorrowfully. "That poor girl was dragged rather than brought up. It comes from having no mother, you know."

"I am only glad that none of my girls act that way," Mrs. Hunt sniffed.

"None of your girls has Lydia's looks or title," Mrs. Leigh said complacently. She clucked her tongue again. "Five daughters, you see," she said to Mrs. Parrot and Augusta.

"At least I—" Mrs. Hunt started to say, but Augusta interrupted.

"Have you any news of the carriage accident last night in Sea Cross?" she asked.

Both ladies turned to look at her with impassive eyes. "I thought that it might have been Alfred, when first I heard," Mrs. Leigh said, "so I sent my footman down to the doctor's house immediately. Happily, it was not Alfred, but another young emigre who used to come and visit him here." She sniffed eloquently.

"Not a very proper sort of person at all,"

Mrs. Hunt put in. "Georges Lamballe." She made a moue of distaste.

"A loose screw," Mrs. Leigh hissed, and Augusta and Mrs. Parrot nodded, although probably not with the horror that was, in the end, expected of them. "A very vulgar sort of person, as some of those emigres unfortunately were."

"There's a bad apple in every barrel," Mrs. Hunt said philosophically.

"One cannot imagine what he was doing in this neighborhood. After all, since de Hasard went back to France nearly a year ago, there's really no reason for him to be here, is there?"

"I certainly would have been forced to snub Lamballe. Not the right sort at all. If you ask me, he was criminal."

Just as Augusta was about to recount their experiences with the gentleman in the phaeton, as if by mutual consent, both ladies rose at once and took their leave.

"What a ruthless pair of females," Augusta exclaimed, going into peals of laughter as soon as the door was closed behind them.

"But I think, in this small circle, very dangerous to offend," Mrs. Parrot remarked, looking up hopefully as Crockett entered the room bearing a luncheon tray. "I do hope there will be scones," she said to the butler, and Augusta found that she was suddenly feeling very hungry indeed.

"This afternoon, I thought we might wish to stroll upon the beach, since the weather has

turned out so well today," Mrs. Parrot said,
and Miss Webb, in the interests of cold ham
and Colby cheese, and, yes, scones for lunch,
dismissed the matter of the mysterious
Frenchman, if not the matter of Mr. Darnley,
from her mind.

7

"I think I could very easily be a man in love," the major announced over the breakfast table.

Augusta, picking absently at a piece of toast, looked up at her brother, who was happily consuming scrambled eggs, kidneys, ham, tomatoes, and muffins, all washed down with cups of strong coffee.

She raised an eyebrow. "Your appetite hardly seems to be that of a man in the throes of his first grand passion," she remarked, watching a little jealously as he smeared a great deal of currant jam over the last muffin and consumed it with a great deal of enthusiasm.

William looked at his sister's plate and shook his head. "I say, seriously, Goose, she is smashing, isn't she?" he asked.

"She is very . . . lively," Augusta said tactfully, and sipped at her tepid chocolate. "Other than that, since I have only been with Lady Towson for about an hour, I could not say. Whatever makes you think you're in love

at last? Not that I am teasing you, mind, Billy,
but really, one would like to know how a
twenty-four-hour acquaintance could have
ripened so soon."

"You have only to see her on a horse," the
major replied somewhat dreamily, and his
sister was forced to conceal her smile behind
her chocolate cup. "What a bruising rider she
is! What a dashed good seat! What hands!"

"I seem to have missed all of that yester-
day, while I was entertaining the good Mrs.
Leigh of the Grange and Mrs. Hunt of the
Larches!"

Billy winced. "Better not to have seen them,
from what you've said. I say, Goose, must we
really go and dance attendance upon those
two old tabbies you describe?"

"If Mrs. Parrot says we must, then we
must," Augusta sighed.

"Well, Lydia—that is, Lady Towson—says
they're always at dagger's drawn over everything, each one about to claw out the other's
eyes in their efforts to become the reigning
hostess of Sea Cross."

"Oh, it's Lydia, now, is it?" Augusta asked,
much amused.

"When one's heart is engaged, one does not
stand upon ceremony," the major said with
vast dignity, dabbing at his face with the
corner of his napkin. "And speaking of Lydia,
Goose, I would very much like to know what
passed between you and Mr. Darnley back at
Niepert. After all, if things should take their

normal course, and I should make an offer for Lydia—"

"An *offer*?" Augusta demanded, stunned.

Billy shrugged. "Well, you see, when it finally happens, one just knows it, Goose. At least that is how I feel."

"And how do you think Lydia will feel?"

The major smiled. "You may ask her that yourself, for she will be coming by this morning. We're all going to ride, you see. She has a mount for you."

"Oh!" Augusta said, not in the least enlightened. "Well, I am certain I thank her for her generosity, but perhaps I might have liked some warning so that I could have planned accordingly?"

"Well, I know *you* wouldn't have anything to do, and I think you and Lydia ought to get to know each other, don't you?"

"Very likely, if you have quite decided that you intend to marry Lady Towson, when you have only known each other twenty-four hours!"

"Well, she don't know it yet. I think it's better not to rush into these things, don't you?" the major asked naively. For once, Augusta was nonplussed, but he continued onward, in all seriousness. "Anyway, that's why I would like to know what's between you and Mr. Darnley. After all, he is her guardian, and I don't think he would take a fancy to me offering for Lydia if there were anything havey-cavey between you two."

Not for the first time, Miss Webb yearned for the presence of Mrs. Parrot, but that lady had departed quite early for a provisioning trip to Rye with Crockett, and was not expected to return until suppertime. However, the major was gazing expectantly at his sister, so she propped her chin in her hands and gazed thoughtfully down at the table-cloth.

"Well, I think you were away at school when I first met Colonel Darnley, as he was then," she said thoughtfully. "At one of the garrison dances. He was above all things a marvelous dancer," she sighed. "Of course I was a mere chit, just out of the schoolroom, you see, and not at all used to being around suitors. And he was very dashing, you see. In short, we were very young and we fancied that we were very much in love."

"You? In love? Goose!" the major said, stunned at the very thought.

"Well, I was, and so was he—at least I thought he was . . . Well, you know Papa. To make a long story short, Darnley's prospects were not great. He was a younger son, of course, and had only a little money, and Papa forbade it."

"Papa was a bit of a Roman tyrant," the major said unemotionally.

"Papa was a—" Augusta started to say, and then stopped, shaking her head. "You are quite right. Papa was quite Roman perhaps more with his daughter than his son. It was

very much a case of 'do as I say, not as I do'
with him, so you may imagine how well he
received Mr. Darnley's proposal. I was for-
bidden to see him again, of course—and of
course I did. I was *not* a dutiful daughter,
Billy." She looked up at her brother with
speaking eyes, and he nodded, full of understanding.

"Well, it was very trying for Mrs. Parrot,
too, you know. I literally had to deceive both
her and Papa to meet Robert—Mr. Darnley—
and it was agreed that we would elope upon a
certain day. Well, I waited and I waited and I
waited, but he never appeared, and my heart,
I thought, was broken, particularly when I
discovered he had been transferred out that
very day. But I assure you it healed very soon
afterward—or so I had thought . . . until I saw
Mr. Darnley again for the first time in over a
decade yesterday."

There was a long silence, broken only when
Billy whistled. "It all sounds very much like
Papa," he said at last. "You may depend upon
it, when all is said and done, you will find
Papa's hand in there somewhere. So that was
what all the stink was about! I was far too
young to know, back then. I only recall the
trouble."

"Well, there you have it," Augusta sighed.
"Doubtless, it may seem strange now, but I
assure you, at the time I believed my life was
ruined."

"And Darnley has never offered you any
explanation of his failure to appear?"

"No, never. It was as if he had disappeared off the face of the earth. Later, of course, I found out that he had done no such thing, but had been ordered to London. However, at least I might have received a letter."

Whatever the major was about to say would never be known, for at that moment, there was a rapping on the french doors leading to the patio, and Lady Towson, in a well-worn riding habit of blue broadcloth, stepped into the room, holding up her loop as she did so. "Good morning," she said, her attention almost entirely upon pulling her skirts through the door behind her. "I hope I do not make myself rude, coming in this way, but my groom is outside with the horses and it is such a lovely day that I could not resist—"

"Good morning, Lady Towson," Augusta interrupted, rising from the table with a speaking look at her brother. "As you can see, I am not yet ready to ride, for my odious brother failed to inform me of the expedition until several minutes ago. If you will be so good as to wait for ten minutes, I shall change and join you presently."

"Ah, Lydia," Billy said, looking adoringly up at Lady Towson. Neither of them seemed to notice Augusta's exit from the room, and when she returned in the promised space of time, it was to find Lady Towson and Billy seated together at the table, gazing at each other over the remains of the buttered toast, so oblivious to anything save each other that they barely heard Augusta enter.

"... always think that a good breakfast is the most important meal of the day, do you not agree, Major?" Lady Townson was saying. "Particularly if one is hunting that day, for one is liable to arrive home so exhausted that all one wants is a cup of tea and one's bed, you know. But, of course, you must, for you say that you hunt with the—Oh, Miss Webb, what a simply glorious habit," Lady Towson interrupted herself to gaze adoringly up at Augusta, attired for the outing in a habit of scarlet merino, cut very much in the military style, with gold nipping and frogs. "How very fashionable you look. Do you suppose when I go to London I shall look so fashionable?" she asked.

"I think you look simply wonderful," the major said, and was rewarded with a sunshine smile.

"I wish that I did, but this habit is only from Rye and quite a year old, besides being much the worse for hard wear," Lady Towson sighed, beaming at him.

Augusta, who was a docile rather than a bruising rider, was pleased to note that Lady Towson was accompanied by her groom, Kirby, a stolid-looking individual who appeared to be devoted to his young mistress's interests. He took one look at Miss Webb and nodded in satisfaction at Lady Towson's choice of a rather gentle mare named Artemis as her mount. It was also immediately clear to Miss Webb that the major stood in good stead with the groom, for he was greeted with a gruff informality by Kirby and urged not to allow Miss Lydia to pull any of her nasty tricks on him, such as charging off at a gallop on the downs.

Thus mounted, they were soon on their way, Kirby trailing a respectful distance behind and Lady Towson chattering a mile to a minute to her guests.

"I thought we might have a tour of the estates today. That way you will always know your own way about, you see. The landscaping was laid out by Capability Brown, but I fear it has been sadly neglected in recent years, for Papa preferred to put his money into the stables, as you will soon see. Robert thinks it is outrageous, but I think he fails to see how very important horses are to one."

"Mr. Darnley is a very good rider," Augusta said as they passed single-file along a path on the cliffs above the sea. She shaded her eyes against the sun and peered out across the water.

"Spain is just across the water," Lady Towson remarked. "At least that is what my nurse always used to say."

"Actually, I believe France is just across the water," Augusta remarked, amused and exasperated.

"Fancy that, France! Yes, I suppose it must be. I am glad that I never knew that when I was little, or I should have suffered the most dreadful nightmares, I am sure, for I was quite terrified of Bonaparte, rather like Griselda was terrified of the headless monk."

"Griselda?" Augusta asked absently. "Oh, yes, Griselda, in one of my books or the other."

Lydia threw her a slightly reproachful look. "It was *The Haunted Castle*, Miss Webb," she said.

"Why, yes, I suppose it was," Augusta murmured. "When one writes as many books as I have, somehow they all begin to blend together."

"I had not thought of that. If I were to only write one book, it would be a minor miracle, I am sure. How much I admire you and your ability to produce such wonderful stories. I quite dote upon your tales, you know."

"You are very kind." Augusta smiled.

Lydia shook her head. "Oh, but not at all! I am very honest. You only need ask Robert and he will tell you that my wretched tongue runs away with me."

"Mr. Darnley is inclined to be a harsh judge," Billy said loyally.

"Well, I think it must be hard upon him, you know, for he knows no more about the ways of young girls than I do about old men of forty."

"Mr. Darnley is not old," Augusta said, rather shocked.

"If you say so, ma'am," Lydia agreed doubtfully. "Anything you say, I shall attend to eagerly, for I cannot tell you how very exciting it is to have one's absolute favorite authoress residing in one's park." She turned an adoring gaze upon Augusta, who merely smiled.

"And that's Seaview Hall, Goose," the major said, pointing with his crop toward the rise ahead where the great house stood above the trees on its own rise of land overlooking the sea. Augusta was inclined to think it was not an attractive house at all, as it was quite similar to the cottage, an unhappy melange of Elizabethan and Jacobite styles, but she managed to sound complimentary when she pronounced it "interesting."

"Yes, I suppose that it is," Lydia replied thoughtfully. "One never thinks of it as anything but home, really, and it is going to rack and ruin for lack of money to keep it up, but there you have it! Now, I must show you the stables. They are of a far greater interest, as I am certain you will agree." So saying, she spurred her horse onward, and the major, in his haste to keep up with her, followed suit. The groom, ever vigilant over Lady Towson, followed close behind them, leaving Augusta to meander in that direction as best she could.

She had just crossed the gravel path between the boxwoods when she heard a familiar voice calling her name, and looked up to see Mr. Darnley in his shirtsleeves, leaning out a lower-story window.

"Have they left you behind, then?" he called, shaking his head.

"I fear I am in no rush to tour the stables," Augusta retorted, laughing.

"Wait there," he cried, and in a moment, he turned the corner of the house, pulling on his coat as he approached her. "I cannot believe that a tour of the stables is not exactly what you would desire," he exclaimed, looking up at her from beneath his eyebrows, his eyes sparkling. He shook his head. "I fear my lady has no more sense of how to go on than a babe unborn. Would you care to come into the house? I should be very pleased to give you the tour—and there are other things I believe we might wish to discuss," he added in a low voice, taking the reins from Miss Webb's fingers and leading her docile mount around to the front of the house.

Before she could protest, he was lifting her out of the saddle and lowering her to the ground, and she noticed, to her own great consternation, that the feeling of his arms about her waist was no less pleasant to her now than it had been a decade before, bringing two bright spots of color into her cheeks.

"Really!" she managed to say. "There *is* a mounting block—"

"My way is easier," he said gruffly, tying the mare unceremoniously to a ring in the portico and guiding her with a firm hand into the cool stone entrance hall.

"Welcome to the home of my mother's

ancestors," Mr. Darnley said, leading her across the cool stone paving toward the enormous fireplace, where an ancient shield and halberd hung above the mantlepiece. "I am certain that you will find something to interest you here, particularly if you like dry rot and crumbling old furniture."

"Do I detect a note of sarcasm in your voice?" Augusta asked, drawing off her gloves and looking about herself at the vaulted ceilings.

"My own home in Hampshire is not quite so grand as all of this, but it is at least in better repair. That I would take a great deal of pleasure in showing you, but this . . ." He grimaced. "I cannot tell you how much it pains me to see it all fall to disrepair, all for the want of a little care and attention. The Towsons have always been far more interested in throwing their income away with both hands than putting it back into their estates. You will note the medieval weapons above the fireplace. I believe they were used by one of my ancestors to kill a great many persons at Agincourt. Unhappily, there is no portrait of him in the gallery, but you may see a great many other unsavory types there."

"Oh, dear," Augusta said in mock distress, but Mr. Darnley was already leading her down the corridor.

"And these are the public rooms," he said, passing briskly through a series of chambers that opened one on the other, where furniture was shrouded in holland covers and great chandeliers draped and darkened. "You can see what it all must have been like in the old lord's—my grandfather's—day. He entertained on a rather large scale, and was a crony of Prince Frederick's. I do not know if my cousin entertained Prinny here, but I would imagine so. Brummell was said to have admired the red salon particularly, I understand. So, we have the red salon, the gold salon, the green salon, and the hall of mirrors here." They passed through a corridor where their reflections met them on either side, and Augusta adjusted her hat. "And then we come into the state dining room."

"Goodness," Augusta said, looking about at the black-and-white floors of Italian marble, the chipped gilt pediments, and the vast dining-room table, which she touched with a finger, leaving a mark in the dust. "I daresay you could seat forty here, if you wanted."

"Sixty, with all the leaves put in. The Duke of Marlborough counted the placements, I believe," Darnley said carelessly. "And now, if you will come along with me, we shall see the galleries."

With a purposeful stride, he walked down another corridor. "It's all a great hodgepodge. My mother's people were great adders-on and builders, so that only the main structure of the house is actually Tudor, and all that's left of the Tudor influence is the hall and the state bedroom, where Queen Elizabeth slept. Since she is said to have traveled with an entourage of about a hundred people, I have no idea where they were all put, but they could have all slept in the state bed quite comfortably." He climbed up a flight of marble stairs and gestured about him as Augusta caught up. "The state bedrooms. This"—he opened a door—"is where Elizabeth slept."

Augusta looked at the huge bed. "Very ornate," she pronounced it.

"Yes, but don't touch the hangings. They're quite rotten and no doubt full of moths. Also, I have a suspicion that the sheets haven't been changed since the day Good Queen Bess left. I wish I could show you the silver furniture, but it's all been melted down to pay my grandfather's debts. Probably just as well, too—it sounds very cold, sitting on silver. Now, this is a series of lesser bedrooms. I believe Charles the Second used one of these rooms at some point or another in his travels. I wish I could say we had a ghost, but it would seem you have the only one. My crazed great-aunt is supposed to walk the corridors, you know, at Seaview Cottage, which was used as a dower house till those damned French cousins took it over . . . Ah, my dear Augusta, you are in for a treat—my ancestors!"

"Ah, the portrait gallery," Augusta exclaimed as they passed along the corridor that opened up above the dining room.

"Yes, and a precious lot they are, too!" Mr. Darnley grimaced. "This is our Tudor

Towson, and the companion piece is his wife.
His first wife. He is rumored to have had
three, you know, and to have murdered them
all."

"Holbein," Augusta judged, peering closely
at the canvases, darkened with age. "What an
unhappy sort he looks to be, quite glum."

"Yes, but look at his wife. I daresay living
with that Friday-faced creature would throw
anyone into the hips."

"But this is their son, this Van Dyke."

"He looks quite smug, I think."

"As well he ought, he married a great
heiress, this blond lady, and managed to
survive Cromwell."

"*She* looks like Lydia, I think."

"And here is their daughter, the first Lady
Towson. Charles the Second made certain of
that. He rather liked Towsons, and I think she
rather liked him."

"And this is their child? I mean, Lord and
Lady Townson's child, for she must have had
a husband."

"A child like Old Rowley himself, you will
notice. Now, he grew up and that is him in
that family group there."

"Goodness, what a great many children
they had! Is that the view from the south
lawn, looking down toward the sea, as you
come from the cottage?"

"Yes, indeed. You are as observant as
always, Augusta. That young man with the
setter bitch was my grandfather, and the little

girl with the frilled cap and the doll became
Lady Hardgrave."

"The political hostess?"

"The same. She was the great friend of Mr.
Pitt, you know."

"Here is your grandfather again, I think.
This must have been painted when he was on
his grand tour—and this is surely Italy."

"Correct. How odd he looks, you know, in
his brocade coat. Atelier Baldini, I believe. It
was quite the thing to do."

"Then these must be his children, in these
two miniatures. How very cherubic they both
look!"

"Angelica Kauffman. Some of her earlier
work, but quite pretty, I think. That smiling
little miss was my mother, clutching that
bird, and the sullen little boy is my uncle,
who, as you can see in this next picture,
became quite blue-chinned and dissipated.
Probably the Stewart blood, you know."

"Oh, it runs in the best families, I am told,"
Augusta said airly, moving on to peer at
another large oil.

"And here we have my cousin George,
Lydia's father, when he had just come into the
title. A Reynolds, but not a very good one, I
fear. Doubtless my cousin was a restless
sitter."

"And here is a kit-kat of Lydia and her
mother. What a charming portrait."

"Maria Cosway—or was it Richard? I can
never recall," Darnley said indifferently.

"Whatever it was, there you have it. When Lydia makes her come-out, I shall have Lawrance do her up properly, of course."

"She is a very pretty girl, you know."

"Yes, I know, but her want of conduct makes her sometimes less attractive to me. Will you come downstairs now? I think we have seen pretty much all that is worthy of viewing. You will forgive me for dragging you through a series of indifferent family portraits and a collection of rotting furniture, but as you can see, my cousin allowed this house to fall into rack and ruin. George was far more interested in events at Brighton and Carleton House than at home—including Lydia's education and upbringing."

"It is all very interesting," Augusta protested. "One can always find something in the houses of others from which to draw some writing."

"So I have noticed." Darnley smiled.

"You've read my work?" Augusta asked, half-astonished.

"The only novels I've ever read, my dear Miss Webb. And let me tell you, *The Specter of Lyndhurst* is *not* a book to be undertaken lightly. It kept me awake all night."

"Reading?"

"No, quivering in fear! Your talent for the macabre is something special, Augusta. You quite surprise me."

She was still laughing as they entered the library.

Looking about at the moldering volumes and the shabby furnishings of the library, Augusta was forced to agree with him. Indicating a chair, he lowered himself into one opposite her and studied her face for a moment, his own countenance unsmiling. "You have changed very little," he said at last, "and in the ways you have changed, you are much improved."

"Your manners at least have suffered no improvement," Augusta countered, drawing off her gloves and placing them inside her riding toque. "Nor has your dress, I might add."

Since Mr. Darnley was carelessly attired in buckskin breeches and high top boots, a Belcher neckcloth tied carelessly about his throat, he only laughed ruefully. "Military neatness was never my forte, I fear," he recalled, placing a hand against his chin, his eyes dancing, before his expression suddenly turned serious. "Augusta, about that night, there is something I must tell you. And I realize that you have every right to be absolutely furious with me."

"It is hard to cherish anger for ten years, Robert," Augusta said slowly, picking at the stitching in her flox gloves, not looking at him at all. "But still, I must admit that even after ten years, there still remains a vestigial curiosity about what happened."

Mr. Darnley shifted uncomfortably in his chair. It was his turn to avert his eyes, and as he spoke, he looked out the window toward the sea, where diamonds of light danced upon the waves. "I always thought that your father had told you," he began.

"Told me what?"

Slowly, he turned to look at her. "You mean you never knew?"

"Perhaps I suspected—yes, somehow I always knew that Papa had a hand in it all," Augusta admitted. "But it was only long after he was dead that I could admit it to myself."

"Well, it was all a very long time ago," Robert said. "Doubtless if we had managed to get to Gretna Green, by now we would have made each other thoroughly miserable!"

"Oh, no doubt about it," Augusta said meaningfully.

Robert smiled at her, much relieved. "Then, you do understand?"

"Of course, and you also?"

"Absolutely."

"Well, I am very happy that we have resolved that after so many years!"

"Oh, yes! And now we may be friends?"

"Indeed, friends! Old friends!"

"That is good, for I have something I must needs ask of you."

"Oh, indeed," Augusta said. "And what might that be?"

Mr. Darnley rose from the chair and paced about the worn carpet in the library, pushing a hand through his dark hair. "It's my ward," he sighed. "Lord knows, it isn't an easy thing for an old bachelor of my age to be saddled with a chit like Lydia—she's been brought up rather badly, as I am sure you've noticed." He smiled ruefully. "Well, I'm sure she's told you all about the late Lord Towson. A dashed loose fish—far more than she knows! Things have been left in a very bad condition indeed—my cousin neglected everything most shockingly, and I daresay it will take years to bring it about again, but with hard work and economy, it can be done!"

"That is indeed fortunate for Lydia," Augusta remarked. "One would hate to see her suffer for things that are none of her fault."

"Ah, but that's not the worst of it! I will admit that some people feel she's a charming, artless sort of a creature, but dealing with the problems of bringing the estate to rights again is nothing compared to the problem of dealing with a headstrong hoyden who's been raised by servants and allowed to do precisely as she wishes from the day she was born. Oh, I'll admit that the people here have always had her best interests at heart. There's not a person on the staff of this house who wouldn't lay down his or her life for Lady Towson, but they've cosseted her and petted her, and no one's ever said her no in her entire life, nor given her the least sense of how to go on, nor installed any sense of propriety or manners into her. My cousin only sent her off to that school in Bath so that he could bring his high fliers down here."

"Sad," Augusta agreed.

"Well, I was hoping that you would say that, because it's clear to me that she looks up to you, and I was hoping, Augusta, that you—"

"Oh, no! I am no preceptress," Augusta protested with a laugh. "Please, do not even think of it."

"Oh, no, not *you*," Mr. Darnley said quickly. "Mrs. Parrot! I was wondering if you could intercede with Mrs. Parrot for me. Surely she can turn this lump of clay into a statue."

"Mrs. Parrot," Augusta exclaimed, falling back into her chair.

"Yes," Robert agreed fervently. "Don't you see, Mrs. Parrot would be perfect to guide Lydia along the right path. Good God, Augusta, if you knew the sorts of things that the girl grew up with ... Well, it is only fortunate that the estate passes through the female line, for her father squandered everything but her inheritance from her mother and the entails, and those French cousins —the de Hasards—who used to live in the cottage were a most ramshackle family. One can only thank God that they went back to France with the Hartwell set."

"Ah, there you are," Lady Towson exclaimed, coming into the room. "We are so sorry you missed the stables."

"They are most interesting," the major said, right behind her. "Very modern! Every convenience!"

"Robert, you must come out and ride with us. You cannot conceive of how beautiful the

day is, nor how stuffy it is to sit in the house,"
Lydia commanded.

"We will continue our talk later," Mr.
Darnley promised in an aside to Augusta.
Aloud, he teased her, with a smile, "What say
you, Miss Webb? Shall I put aside these dull
account books and farming journals and take
advantage of this fine weather?"

"I think it would be very nice if you did,"
she replied, meeting his eyes before dropping
her gaze in slight confusion at what she saw
written there.

Mr. Darnley shrugged his shoulders and
stretched his arms. "What say you, Major
Webb? Could you stand another male about
these two females?"

"Oh, I think it would be a capital idea, and
so does Goose," the major said quickly, very
anxious to please.

"Then I shall play truant," Mr. Darnley
announced.

"Well, you do not see me bent over my
work," Augusta admitted with a laugh.

"Then it is settled," Lydia exclaimed.
"Come, we are going to ride up to the old
smuggler's cave. I am determined that the
Webbs shall see all that is interesting in our
neighborhood."

"We have all of six months to visit everything," Augusta promised.

"Then doubtless you will want to sail on my
yacht before the weather turns too crisp. I
keep her in Rye, at the harbor. I will take you

there one day," Mr. Darnley promised her as they all walked down toward the stables.

"I think I would find that very interesting. And so would Billy," Augusta said, feeling a little more comfortable with him. "I have never set foot aboard a boat before in my life, you know."

"Goose, don't exaggerate! You punted when I was up at Oxford," Billy reminded her.

Augusta laughed. "Well, that can hardly be said to count, can it?" she asked.

"Most people in these parts are born on boats," Lydia said over her shoulder. "I cannot see it, myself. Give me a good horse and dry land any day of the week."

"Lydia suffers from *mal de mer*," Mr. Darnley said, shaking his head as if the idea that anyone could ever be seasick were totally alien to his thinking. "Ah, Kirby! Would you be good enough to saddle up the bay gelding for me? Then I doubt if we'll want you for the rest of the afternoon. Miss Lydia will be in thoroughly good hands, I assure you," he said to the groom as they approached.

The man turned his currycomb in his hand and shot Mr. Darnley a look from beneath his heavy eyebrows. "Happens where Miss Lyddie goes, I go," he said stubbornly. "I promised the old lord."

Lady Towson, explaining the finer points of the improvements made in the stalls by her father to Augusta, seemed to ignore this interchange, but it did not slip past Miss Webb, who noted the way in which Mr. Darnley's lips thinned out and his dark eyes flashed displeasure.

However, Mr. Darnley made no further protest, and the five of them departed from the stables in a very short time, John Kirby following the two couples at a respectful distance.

Lydia, who seemed to be well versed in the history of her inheritance and her neighborhood, chattered on as they wound their way through the bridle paths in the park, and Augusta listened with half an ear, enjoying the beauty of the weather and the crispness of the day. She was amused to note the way in which her brother seemed to hang on to every word of Lady Towson's, however, and looked over once to see Mr. Darnley grinning at her in a most devilish sort of way.

"Your brother seems properly smitten by my ward," he murmured beneath his breath.

"I think he must be," Augusta admitted. "He announced this morning at breakfast that he was in love. Of course, when one is so young, it always seems that way, every time," she could not resist adding.

If her barb found the target, Mr. Darnley gave no notice, for his smile did not waver. "He must have a decided *tendre* for her, if he can put up with her ceaseless prattle for hours upon end. I find it tiring, to say the least!"

"Lady Towson is certainly very full of words," Augusta observed.

"And not a thought in her head to rub

against another one," Mr. Darnley sighed. "I was never one for silly women."

"No, you were not. But Lydia is not silly—merely a chatterbox."

"A very silly schoolroom miss—the sort of female I cannot book! Which I would suppose would go a long way to explaining why I am a bachelor still. But what has kept you in a state of blessed singleness?"

Augusta shrugged her shoulders. "Perhaps I could never tolerate silly men," she suggested, and to cover her confusion galloped on ahead, Darnley's laughter ringing in her ears.

Their expedition to see the snug little beach head cave where the dreaded Hawkhurst gang had landed their cargoes in the heyday of smuggling accomplished, together with a great many bloodcurdling tales of that infamous crew, the party returned by the road, as it was getting on toward noon.

"Oh, Lord," Lydia said as a curricle approached from the opposite direction. "Here comes Mrs. Leigh. Now we are in for it."

"I don't suppose there's anywhere we can hide, is there?" the major asked, only half in jest, looking about at the hedgerows as if he expected them to be able to swallow him up.

"No, and I wish there were! The only thing worse would be encountering Mrs. Hunt," Darnley sighed. "They are our neighbors, you know, and a more competitive pair of females

would be hard to find. Now we shall be
cornered into it, wait and see."

"I have made their acquaintance. They
called on us yesterday," Augusta said.

"Then I need not tell you what a pair of lion-
hunters they are." Mr. Darnley shook his
head.

However, the curricule was upon them.
Mrs. Leigh, today enshrouded in a many-
caped driving cloak and a hat seeming to be
entirely composed of artificial cherries,
tapped her coachman with her parasol in
order to stop and raise her lorgnette to her
eyes. "Well," she said. "I see that you are all
going along very well."

If there was a faint hint of jealousy in her
voice, they were all able to ignore it as they
murmured polite greetings.

"I do not believe you have met my brother,"
Augusta said. "Mrs. Leigh, may I present
Major Webb?"

"I had heard that your brother was with
you," Mrs. Leigh said. "And I am very pleased
to make your acquaintance, Major! Please
allow me to give you a few words of advice,
although I would certainly never dream of
thrusting myself forward."

"Advice, ma'am?" the major asked,
genuinely puzzled.

All the artificial cherries nodded at once.
"Do not, young man, allow Mrs. Hunt to hear
of your presence, or you shall have no peace,
no peace at all!"

"Mrs. Hunt? I do not believe I know the lady," Billy said uncertainly, and Lydia had to press a glove against her lips to stifle her laughter.

"Daughters, my dear young man! Daughters," Mrs. Leigh said, quivering with indignation. "Four of them to launch, and all of them bracket-faced! No doubt she will ask you to come to her country dance on Friday, but you would all do much better to be at the Grange that night for a comfortable sort of supper and cards! I have no daughters! Miss Webb, always a pleasure. Dear Lydia, Mr. Darnley!" She poked at her coachman with the end of her parasol and drove on in a cloud of dust.

"D-daughters?" the major asked, looking after her.

"Daughters!" Lady Towson promised him. "And although I would never want to appear to agree with anything Mrs. Leigh would say, I must admit that they are all remarkably unattractive creatures! And dull as dishwater, too!"

The major was nonplussed, even when Augusta and Darnley had burst into laughter. "I think I had best explain to you about our neighbors, Mrs. Leigh—"

"—of the Grange," Lydia said.

"And Mrs. Hunt—"

"Of the Larches," Augusta added gloomily.

"Yes, I think you better had," the major

agreed, looking over his shoulder as if he
expected a horde of bracket-faced Hunt
daughters to come in pursuit of him from out
of the bushes.

8

"Well," said Augusta as she descended the stairs, fresh from the hands of Polestack, "do I look as if I am going to the tumbrils? I certainly *feel* that way."

Mrs. Parrot, in her conservative mauve silk trimmed with black lace, looked up from her tatting in approval. "I think that will do very nicely, my dear. After all, a party at Mrs. Leigh's is hardly the same as a party in London."

"Well do I know that," Augusta said, making a face as she regarded herself critically in the mirror above the mantel. "I only fail to see why, when everything has been going so very well, we must interject our-selves in to the lion's den."

"Only consider how very disappointed William would be if we had cried off. After all, Lady Towson is particularly anxious to attend, and they are to take us in their carriage."

Augusta thrust a tiny foot, encased in a delicate slipper of striped satin, out from beneath the hem of a jonquil peau-de-soie gown, richly trimmed in Venice lace, and frowned. "I can understand that she does not have many opportunities to appear socially, since she has been in mourning for nearly a year, and a year is a very long time for a very young girl, but I fear we shall find it all a dead bore, Parry."

"Very likely, my dear Augusta, it will not at all suit our notions of a lively evening, but, after all, these are our neighbors now, and we must at least appear civil. Besides, I do feel we owe it to Mr. Darnley, do you not?"

Augusta bit her lower lip and lowered her eyes. "Yes, very likely," she agreed reluctantly. "Even I must admit that he has shown us nothing but kindness since we took possession of the cottage. Certainly the ghost stories and folk tales he has elicited from the locals for me have been of a great help in commencing *Horrida*. Imagine, I did five whole pages today before breakfast."

"And you have certainly enjoyed your morning rides with him, as well as the cruises he has been so kind as to provide for us aboard his yacht. Nothing could have been more generous nor more considerate than his attentions toward us, and toward William. I must say fresh air and salubrious exercise have greatly improved his health, and for that, we must acknowledge our debt to Mr. Darnley," Mrs. Parrot pointed out.

"Oh, yes, he has been everything that is kind," Augusta admitted.

"Then we can certainly not, in all good conscience, allow ourselves to be remiss in attending Lydia's first grown-up dance."

Augusta was forced to acknowledge the truth of this, but she could not help but add, "Yes, but I am afraid any and all credit for her must rest upon your shoulders. Certainly you have been far more instrumental in preparing her for this occasion than I, dearest Parry."

"I will admit," Mrs. Parrot replied, "that a hint or two dropped in the child's ear concerning proper conduct of a lady in a social gathering such as this may not always have fallen upon fertile ground." She frowned slightly. "One can only hope that the rather formidable personality of Mrs. Leigh will restrain her from any sort of schoolgirlish excesses."

"Well, I am fond enough of her, for her own sake, for she is a good-hearted creature, but she will do just as she pleases when it is least convenient," Augusta said doubtfully. "And of course, Billy encourages her. In his eyes, she is all that is delightful."

"Well, better she should act up now than when she is in London," Mrs. Parrot said, tatting away.

"I say, are you all ready?" the major asked, limping into the room, resplendent in his best dress uniform. "By Jove, you both look smashing."

Mrs. Parrot merely smiled, but Augusta rearranged his black stock to better suit herself.

"Well, one month here, and already I can see the change in you, Billy," she remarked affectionately, pinching his cheek. "I do believe that country air is well nigh to restoring you completely to yourself."

"I do feel better," the major admitted, turning to draw back the curtains to peer into the night. He glanced at the clock on the mantelpiece. "Shouldn't they be arriving soon?" he asked impatiently.

"Very soon," Mrs. Parrot said, and at that moment, the sound of carriage wheels in the driveway was heard.

In a very few minutes, Lydia burst into the room, all volubility and light, her cheeks flushed with excitement and her eyes dancing. "Well," she said, "what do you think, now that I am out of mourning and back into colors again?"

She spun about, and the Webbs and Mrs. Parrot were treated to the vision of a young and pretty girl in a gown of palest blue, caught at hem and sleeve with ropes of white silk. About her neck had been clasped a rope of seed pearls, and her dark hair had been piled atop her head, falling in ringlets about her heart-shaped face.

"Very pretty," Mrs. Parrot pronounced, and if Augusta felt an inward relief that the dressmaker in Rye had been dissuaded from indulging in any of the excesses Lydia had imagined, she was far too tactful to say so aloud.

"Indeed, my dear, you look everything that

is becoming," she said with a great deal of approval, and was rewarded with a grateful look for her pains.

"I told her that her choice would be exactly what you would have wished," Mr. Darnley said from the doorway, raising one eyebrow quizzically. "It restrained her from choosing a moire silk gown of deepest purple! Think on it!"

Lydia's expression clouded over. "But it was a beautiful dress," she exclaimed. "You know nothing about female attire, Robert."

"No, he does not," Augusta said quickly, "but you must recall that Mr. Darnley has seen a great deal more of the world than you, and if he says that a purple dress is totally inappropriate, then I am forced to agree. Purple," she added quickly, "is such a dificult color for the best of us, and I am certain that it would make you look quite a quiz, whereas the gown you have chosen is in every way appropriate to you."

"Do you really think so?" Lydia asked, her expression changing into one of hope.

"In general, I have found that young ladies who have not yet made their debuts are generally attired in pastels," Mrs. Parrot put in. "But I can recall a time when Augusta was no more than your age and became enamored of a very shocking dress of the most deplorable shade of puce. It took a great deal of explaining for her to understand how very dismal she would have looked in it, but in the end, she was glad she did not purchase it."

"Yes, if *you* say so," Lydia agreed docilely.

"Well, I think you look beautiful," Billy put in, gazing at her in a rather moonstruck manner. "A vision, if you will!"

He was rewarded with a smile. "Thank you, Billy!" Lydia beamed.

"Well, do you see?" Mr. Darnley asked in a low voice to Augusta. "I spent an afternoon remonstrating with her, and all it took from you was a few simple words."

"That is because you were never a young female," Augusta returned, gazing with admiration at his corbeau-colored evening clothes. He was simply, if elegantly, attired in knee britches and a plainly cut coat that must have come from the hand of Scott, but there was something so distinguished in his appearance that she could not help but feel a surprising admiration for him, and there was something in the way in which he regarded her that made her understand that his feelings toward her were not simply those of a grateful friend.

"Do you intend to dance, Augusta?" he asked. "I shall hope that you shall save at least one for me."

"Oh, indeed," Augusta said, flustered, as much by her own feelings as by the way he pressed her hand into his own.

From the very moment they entered the Grange, Augusta had a very strong feeling that she knew precisely how the evening would be, but she had no way of being able to forecast how the rather speedy exit she hoped to make would be aided by circumstances she could not yet determine.

The Grange, while hardly as large or as imposing as Seaview Hall, was a formidable Palladian structure, and it was clear Mr. and Mrs. Leigh meant to allow their guests to know that they were possessed of a comfortable fortune. Certainly, they were determined to put on a show of elegance, for from the moment that the party's cloaks were retrieved by a footman in a powdered wig until they rose from the supper table, it seemed to Augusta that everything was done in such excess as to make her head spin.

Mr. Leigh, who received them at the side of his large wife, was every bit as formidably overdressed as she. From the large diamond thrust into his neckcloth to the even larger emerald upon his finger it was evident he had done very well by himself in the recent wars, and was anxious to display his bounty in any way possible. The orchestra had been gotten up from London for the event, and a large body of footmen served the numerous courses at the large and stately dinner table. While Mrs. Leigh, resplendent in diamonds and feathers in her hair, sat at the head of the table, he placed Augusta on his right at the foot and did not hesitate to regale her with the price and provenance of every object within sight. If he was disappointed that she had neither the style nor the appearance he might have expected from, as he styled her, the famous literary lady from London, he was just able to conceal his disappointment. However, he did not hesitate to inquire of her precisely what the sums Messieurs Clock and Fishbridge might be expected to lay out for the work of a best-selling authoress, and was very disappointed when Miss Webb said that she did not have any figures to hand.

Nor, she decided, were the rest of the company all that prepossessing. They seemed to have been chosen for their rank in society rather than any claims to congeniality, for when the tables turned and she was forced into an attempt to make conversation with the elderly bishop to her left, after an initial inquiry into her antecedents and a grim exhortation against the writing of novels, he seemed entirely devoted to his food.

Once or twice, she glanced across the centerpiece, an enormous silver epergne filled with fruit and flowers, and caught the sympathetic eye of Mr. Darnley, wedged between one of Mrs. Hunt's bracket-faced daughters and a forbidding dowager of arctic mien wearing a very large diamond tiara.

If this, Augusta thought as the ninth course was placed before her, was Mrs. Leigh's idea of a small country dance, she wondered how it in any way differed from one of the old queen's drawing rooms, save that those royal events were only slightly less formal. She would never stop feeling bemused by provincial manners, she decided, staring glassily at the sorbet that was placed before her by her very own footman between the meat and game courses.

When at last Mrs. Leigh gave the signal to allow the ladies to rise from the table, she felt as if she would burst, for even a polite nibble of the varied dishes set before her had been enough to make her feel quite full, and the wines, at which she had only sipped, had been many and various, while the frothy dessert had been such a concoction of whipped creams, chocolate, spun sugar, and fruit that the mere sight of it had made her feel slightly ill.

"Small country dance indeed," she whispered to Mrs. Parrot as the ladies all clustered in a large and decidedly gilded salon to await the presence of the gentlemen.

"I am afraid that Mrs. Leigh's idea of such a levee is entirely different from our own," Mrs. Parrot returned.

"There!" said Mrs. Hunt, more skeletal than ever in an umber sarcenet gown and a drab shawl, as she settled herself in the narrow space on the couch between Augusta and Mrs. Parrot. "Did you ever see such vulgarity, and all in the most excessive style? Depend upon it, before the evening is out, that odious woman will have claimed to a number of persons that she was the first to discover you in the district, Miss Webb. How she contrives to set up so lavishly, I have no idea, but I can only say that Mr. Leigh's money comes from trade."

"No," Augusta said, quite shocked, but not for the reason Mrs. Hunt had hoped for.

"You may depend when you come to the Larches that nothing will be done with such vulgarity," she continued in tones of self-satisfaction. "Of course, I had to postpone it for a week. But after this, it will seem all the better."

Fortunately, at that moment several of the young ladies of the party began to address themselves to the pianoforte in the corner, and Augusta's struggle for a reply was lost.

"Only look at that poor Lydia," Mrs. Hunt continued, shaking her head. "It is a great deal too bad that she is such a hoyden, for with her very small fortune, and her own title, you may depend upon it that no man will ever look at her. Of course, I brought my Sophie out this year, and doubtless Lydia would have come out, too, if her father had not died." She clucked her tongue.

It occurred to Augusta to remark very loyally that Sophie was a very lucky girl not to be placed in the same year as Lady Towson, since it was evident that the eldest Hunt girl could not bear the competition, but she held her tongue and smiled gently upon the very pretty scene Lydia made as she sang an old country ballad, accompanied by the youngest of the Hunt girls.

She was flushed with excitement, as were

all the young ladies, for whom the advent of a country dance was still enough of a novelty to be a treasured experience, and if she seemed a trifle high-spirited ... well, then, Augusta decided, it was quite natural, given the circumstances, that Lydia should laugh and jest about with her friends. Besides, she noted loyally, it was a simple matter for a normal girl to appear high-spirited in comparison to the Hunt sisters, who, in addition to being bracket-faced, were also deplorably dull-spirited creatures with shining, nasal voices very much like their mother's.

What Augusta could not know was that Lydia, at her first grown-up party, had consumed far more of the many and varied wines than was entirely good for her, and was feeling their effects, combined with the general excitement, quite sharply.

Before either she or Mrs. Parrot could grasp the situation, the gentlemen had joined the ladies.

"You have no idea what I have been subjected to," Mr. Darnley whispered to Miss Webb as he escorted her to the ballroom.

"Try me," she suggested, laughing, before her hand was claimed by an effete young man in a cherry-striped waistcoat for the opening dance.

Since she was something of a novelty in the district, and had been much heralded in advance by her hostess, Augusta found that she did not lack for partners, even if a great many of them were pompous bores who were inclined to tread on her toes and whisper rather risque things into her ears that would have displeased their wives almost as much as they discomfited her.

It was with relief that she found Darnley claiming her hand for the waltz, for she knew of old that he was a skilled and enjoyable dancing partner, and they stepped out into the floor arm in arm.

"How very glad I am to claim you," he said, placing his hand firmly on her waist and looking down at her with such a rueful look on his face that she was forced to laugh. "I have had the privilege—thrust upon me, if you will—of dancing with all the Hunt sisters as well as Mrs. Leigh's rather hopeful daughter-in-law—the one who resembles a cocker spaniel, you know—and have been bored within an inch of my life. Aside from which, the port Mr. Leigh served us is sitting right at my collarbone."

"You never did like port," Augusta remarked as the music commenced and they began to swirl across the floor.

"Do you recall this tune? They played it the night you and I danced at Niepert Garrison for the very first time."

"Oh, yes, Mrs. Parrot had severe doubts about the propriety of me waltzing, but in the end she allowed as how it was a graceful-enough little dance."

"And you were the best dancer I'd ever

seen, in that pink gown with those tea roses in your hair," Mr. Darnley said, his dark eyes shining.

"Oh, but we could have danced all night!" Augusta sighed, shaking her head. "Lord, what a pair of fools we were!"

Darnley's expression became unreadable as he replied, "Oh, yes, a very great pair of fools, smelling all of April and May."

For a few more minutes, they circled the floor amid the other couples in a pleasant silence until, without warning, Darnley cursed under his breath.

"I swear, one of these days I'll kill that chit," he said in a low voice. "Come! I may need your help in this if we are to avoid a scandal." He grasped her hand in his and led her off the floor, toward the terrace.

"Whatever—" Augusta tried to say, but as Darnley flung open the windows that led out on the terrace, she saw the cause of his concern.

"Billy," she said sharply to her brother, who seemed to be holding the supine form of Lydia in his arms, leaning against the stone balustrade, "whatever do you think—"

"I'll see to this," Darnley said grimly, shutting the door behind him and striding across the flagstones. "Good God, Lydia, are you lost to all sense of propriety as to disappear, unescorted, from a dance with a man? This is outrageous."

"It's not what you think it is, Mr. Darnley,"

the major said, taking a faltering step beneath his burden.

Lydia looked up, her head beneath the major's epaulet. Her face was ghastly pale and a silly smile covered her face. " 'Ullo, Robert." She giggled. "Feel most unaccountably—oh!" She sighed and with an upward roll of her eyes collapsed into the major's arms. "I feel rather dizzy."

"It was the wine, I think," the major said apologetically. "She seems to have drunk too much of it. Thought she might be sick, so I got her out here just in time."

"This is a fine thing indeed," Darnley said sternly, his hands on his hips.

Augusta drew her handkerchief out of her reticule and dabbed it against Lydia's perspiring cheeks.

"Oh, Miss Webb," Lady Towson sighed, "I believe I am a trifle foxed, between the wines at dinner and the champagne at the dance."

"So it would seem," Augusta said. "My dear child, when one is unused to wine, it is best to stay away from it all together."

Lydia's only reply was a low moan.

Darnley shook his head. "What a scandal you have created, slipping unescorted out of the ballroom with a man! Good God, girl, is there no end to your hoydenish pranks?"

"It was a natural mistake," the major said. "I thought if she had some fresh air—"

"Fresh air, and the whole room watching you both slip away, I've no doubt," Mr.

Darnley exclaimed, exasperated. "If that damned school in Bath would take you back, I'd ship you there tomorrow."

"You would, would you?" Lydia said angrily. "Of all the gothic, overbearing tyrants, you, sir, are certainly the worst."

"Come, now, Robert, it is nothing, a natural mistake," Augusta said placatingly.

"Anyone but a hoyden with no more upbringing than a scullery maid certainly would have known better," Mr. Darnley said sternly. "You, miss, are a spoiled, headstrong creature without manners or upbringing, and it will be a cold day in hell before I let you out again to make such a scene."

"Go to the devil," Lydia sputtered.

"Here, now, sir! There's no need to put her head out for washing," William interjected.

Whatever Darnley would have replied to that will never be known for at that moment Mrs. Parrot opened the french door and came upon the scene, her placid demeanor by no means ruffled by the scene she witnessed.

"I see that you have imbibed too freely, my dear Lady Towson," she announced calmly, going to the girl's side and placing an arm about her shoulders. "I am not surprised, for certainly persons with a great deal more experience of wine than you seem to be feeling the effects of the numerous vintages offered tonight. Dear Robert, will you be good enough to order the carriage? Augusta, do go find Mrs. Leigh and inform her that Lady Towson has succumbed to the headache that has been plaguing her all night long. William, be so kind as to help me assist Lady Towson to the cloakroom. My dear, do you feel as if you can make an exit without causing undue attention to be directed at yourself?''

"The only thing that is making me ill is that odious guardian of mine, with all his fustian notions," Lydia exclaimed, adding a low moan as a wave of illness seized her.

The ride home was accomplished in silence, punctuated only by Lydia's moans. The major was solicitous and Mrs. Parrot was kept busy employing her vinaigrette. If the truth were to be told, Miss Webb's sympathies were entirely with Mr. Darnley, but that gentleman seemed so entirely wrapped up in his own thoughts that she thought it best not to offer him any conversation.

It was only when they were safe in the house that the major gave vent to his anger. "I say, if ever there was a man less suited to be the guardian of an innocent young girl than Darnley, I cannot think who it would be," he exclaimed, full of indignation. "Too much to drink that's all—could have happened to anyone. Must have brought the entire cellar up tonight."

"Well, she certainly should have known better," Augusta snapped without much patience. "I would not doubt that she has seen the gross effects of wine upon her own father often enough, if he's been one of Prinny's cronies, to know its injurious effects."

"When did you become such a high

stickler?" William demanded hotly. "I think you'd side with Darnley if he were the devil himself, simply because you've never gotten over your *tendre* for him."

Hot spots of color appeared in Augusta's cheeks, and her fingers closed about her reticule strings as if she would have very much liked to have a swing at her brother as they had done in nursery days. "Not true! Not true," she exclaimed.

"Indeed, I think the pair of you are behaving far worse than poor Lady Towson," Mrs. Parrot said evenly. "Perhaps you are both overtired, and should go up to your rooms and prepare for bed."

"Not me," Augusta said irritably, drawing off her gloves. "I have five or six more pages to write before I go to bed. Someone around here must pay the bills." So saying, she flounced away toward the library.

"It is clear to me that Robert is quite correct," Mrs. Parrot said thoughtfully, in no way perturbed by Augusta's behavior. "I must take a hand in poor Lady Towson's education before it drives us all quite over the brink."

9

If anything was seen or heard of the company at Seaview Hall for the next week, Augusta was able to keep herself above it. When pleading the cause of her muse, it was an inviolate rule of the household that she not be disturbed for any reason. Seated at a spacious desk overlooking a beautiful seascape, she set herself to work with a new will, completely immersed in the doings of her rather shatterbrained heroine, Horrida, who had been heartlessly thrust into the clutches of as great a set of villains as she could conceive. She toiled away from breakfast until well past the dinner hour, eating her meals from a tray and making her hours so different from the rest of the household that she saw no one for days on end.

Following this regimen, she was prolific and, toward the end of July, was able to write to Clock and Fishbridge that she had every hope of delivering them a very satisfactory manuscript in as short a time as possible, a piece of news she was fairly certain would cause sighs of relief in those dark and pleasantly musty-smelling offices on Milk Street.

Horrida had just found herself in a locked dungeon, where tidal water was slowly rising over her head, one pleasant sunny morning on a day filled with summer sun, when there was a knock upon the library door and Crockett cautiously thrust his head through the opening.

"You must excuse me, ma'am, but there is a gentleman at the door," he said, looking very much as if he expected to have an inkstand lobbed at his head. "He is very desirous of seeing the lady of the house."

"Mrs. Parrot—" Augusta began, splattering ink across her manuscript and reaching for the shaker.

Crockett shook his head. "Mrs. Parrot is at the Larches, ma'am, something to do with procuring a recipe for chicken-foot jelly."

"Then my brother—"

"Out riding with Lady Towson, ma'am." He coughed discreetly. "The gentleman would appear to be French, ma'am, and was most insistent."

"French?" Augusta repeated, immediately intrigued. "Very well, Crockett, I shall see him in the morning room."

She rose and picked up her cashmere shawl, draping it about the shoulders of her ivory morning dress. With a quick look at her hair in the mirror above the mantelpiece, she hurried, practically agog with curiosity, into the drawing room.

He stood with his back to her, examining a clock upon the mantlepiece, and for a moment she was certain that he was the same man they had encountered in the accident upon the road, for everything about him was in the first style of elegance, from the red heels of his gleaming hessian boots to the burnished pomade of his russet curls, and she gave an involuntary gasp, for she had long believed him dead.

At the sound of her voice, however, he turned, lifting one eyebrow quizzically, and she saw that this was not at all the same person, but a man of such breathtaking handsomeness that even Augusta was rendered, for a moment, speechless.

"Forgive me," he said in English with only the merest trace of French accent. "I am Alfred de Hasard, the cousin of Lady Towson who once upon a time lived in this house."

"Oh, I see," Augusta replied, although she did not at all, and was surprised to find her hand being grasped in a firm grip while the largest pair of chestnut-brown eyes she had ever seen gazing soulfully into her own. She might only have known his nationality by the way in which he was dressed. Such a tightly molded pair of breeches and a coat of lustring blue had never come from the hands of an English tailor, while the ivory-striped waistcoat and ornately tied cravat about his neck had never been seen in a London drawing room, and no Englishman would have sported the thin and well-trimmed mustache that ornamented his upper lip.

"You must forgive me for startling you," he said gently.

Augusta shook her head. "Oh, no, it is only that I thought you were someone else—someone who died."

He sighed, as if apologizing for still being alive. "But I have been so close to death so many times," he murmured, then shrugged, adding, "Like so many emigres, of course."

"I am Augusta Webb," she said quickly. "I am afraid that you will not find any of us at home today save me."

He smiled and nodded with such sadness that Augusta wondered if he were ill, but when he offered no further explanation of his presence, she found herself indicating a chair, into which he sank with a little sigh, withdrawing a handkerchief from his pocket.

As she warily seated herself opposite him, she regarded him with interest, for he was looking about the room.

"You must forgive me," he said at last, "but my childhood was passed in this house. I wanted only to see it one more time before I returned to France."

Although she would have guessed him to be no older than herself, she was somehow surprised that he would express a nostalgia for such a ramshackle place as the cottage. "I suppose," she offered, "that there were a great many emigres settled in this area."

His eyes flickered over her appreciatively and he shook his head. "Oh, no, only Maman and Papa and I. We came because Lady Towson's mother was a cousin of my brother, you see."

"I suppose Lady Towson sent word down from the hall that you would be visiting, but I am sorry that I did not hear of it," Augusta said, wondering if she should offer refreshment.

De Hasard smiled his sad smile and shrugged his shoulders. "I have not yet been to the hall to see my cousin," he admitted. "Her guardian and I do not agree on all points, you see, but I was seized with such an urge to revisit one more time the haunts of my youth before returning to France that I simply took a chance. And you have been so kind," he added.

Augusta judged it was time to send for the tea tray.

"So you are going back to France?" she asked, pouring China tea into Limoges cups.

M. de Hasard accepted his cup with a ravishing smile. "I have already been back," he said. "I went to reclaim my family's estates. My father is gone, of course. He died in this very house of a broken heart, and Maman—well, she lives now at Maison de Hasard among her ghosts." He shrugged his shoulders again and smiled his sweet, sad

smile. "She was lady-in-waiting to poor
Princesse de Lamballe. Witnessed the whole
terrible thing. I fear that, after that, her mind
was never the same."

Augusta shuddered. "I would think not,"
she murmured, placing a half-eaten macaroon
on her plate.

M. de Hasard sighed. "I was of course much
too young to understand it all. Would you
believe that my parents smuggled me out
beneath a cartload of cabbages?"

"It must have been dreadful," Augusta
agreed.

"Well, what can one say? One goes with
fortune, you see. And we were fortunate to
have the cottage, so very fortunate. My cousin
and I played among the rocks on the cliffs,
and we were happy. But of course the late
lord forbade us anything controversial. His
tenants might have gotten ideas. I have not
seen Lydia since she was packed off to Bath.
She was younger than I, but I was always fond
of her."

"And now your rights and lands are
restored to you?"

De Hasard's expression flickered slightly.
"Oh, they have been so for some time," he said
airily. "I am only back *pour la nostalgie*.
Business brought me to London and I thought
that since things were taking so very long to
settle with the lawyers there, I could come
here and visit my cousin."

"But you have not gone to the hall?"

The Frenchman smiled. "I fear Mr. Darnley would not be at all happy to see me. He has never approved of Lydia's emigre relations. And also"—he sipped at his tea—"I am the black sheep of the family." His smile was charming, a denial of his words.

Setting his teacup on the tray, he looked about the room. "So many memories in this old house," he sighed.

"You must allow me to give you a tour, then—or perhaps you will be kind enough to give me a tour," Augusta offered.

M. de Hasard rose to his feet and offered Augusta his arm. "But I would be charmed, dear lady. Tell me, are you *the* Miss Webb, the author of all of those wonderful novels?"

As they strolled through the downstairs rooms, it was in the back of Augusta's mind that her guest evinced only slight interest in the scenes of his youth, and even the discovery of a genuine Plantagenet cabinet beneath a stack of books in the library seemed to elicit only a "very interesting" from his lips, although once or twice he sighed and recalled his parents' woes with a certain degree of feeling.

She saw nothing amiss in his desire to tour the upper story and watched with a certain degree of sympathy as he fondled pieces of bric-a-brac in the rooms that had belonged to his mother, now occupied by Mrs. Parrot.

But when he came to her chambers, a strange sort of light illuminated those chestnut eyes, and he began to tap at the paneling with his knuckles. "This was my room," he said. "How well I recall that carving! Do you know, when I was very small, I sometimes fancied all those Tudor nymphs and satyrs were actually dancing? And worse yet, I fancied that something would come out of there and eat me alive." He laughed at his own folly, but Augusta, remembering her dream, merely frowned.

"In truth, Monsieur de Hasard, the first night I slept here, I awoke in the middle of the night and thought that I saw a figure standing there. Isn't that simply fantastic?"

M. de Hasard looked at her from beneath his long lashes for a moment before allowing himself to smile. "Oh, utterly silly, I know, but old Cooley always used to say that this room was haunted."

As they descended the stairs, they were both laughing, until they caught sight of the figure standing in the hall, glaring reproachfully at M. de Hasard.

"And what, I might ask," Darnley said, his arms folded across his chest, his brows drawn together in a dark look, "are *you* doing back here?"

Before M. de Hasard could reply, Lydia and the major had come through the door, both of them dressed in their riding clothes.

Lady Towson's face lit up with joy and with a squeal she threw herself into de Hasard's arms. "Oh, Alfred, Alfred, Alfred, how much I have missed you!"

10

M. de Hasard, breaking away from Lydia's embrace, held her at arm's length. "*Ma petite cousine*," he exclaimed. "But you are not so little anymore, I see. In fact, you have grown up into quite a young lady."

Lydia flushed with pleasure. "Do you think so?" she asked, much pleased. "I would like to think so, for next Season I will make my London come-out! But how and when did you come? And from where?"

"I am in England for a visit, trying to settle my affairs here before setting my estates in France to rights. How do you do, Darnley?"

"De Hasard," he said without enthusiasm, nodding abruptly before going across the room to stand behind Augusta.

"And this is my great friend, Major Webb, and I see you have met Miss Webb. And where is Mrs. Parrot? You must meet Mrs. Parrot, she is ciceroning me through all of the very rigid things one must learn if one is to be accomplished and know everything—"

De Hasard laughed. "I see that you are still

a chatterbox, cousin," he observed, with a little laugh.

"Of course she is," Mr. Darnley observed in a voice heavy with sarcasm. "Lydia keeps us all diverted."

She made a moue at her guardian. "Don't listen to him! Robert is not at all amusing. With him everything must be proper and serious."

"Ah, how well I know," de Hasard agreed. "Major Webb? Major Webb? Of the Fourth Dragoons? I think that I may be acquainted with a Colonel Bagby of that regiment—we were at school together."

Whatever doubts the major might have felt were dissipated. "What? You are a friend of old Sacks and Gloves? Famous!"

"Sacks and Gloves! Yes, a very good nickname for him indeed." De Hasard nodded. "He was forever in the sack . . . But we must continue this talk at a time when there are not ladies present."

"But I want to hear," Lydia exclaimed.

"And I do not," Augusta said firmly. "War stories bore me to tears, Monsieur de Hasard. I would much prefer to hear about how events are progressing with the Restoration."

"But how came you to the cottage?" Lydia asked. "You should have gone at once to the hall, for that was where we all were. You will come and stay with me, will you not? It has been all of five years and more since we last met, cousin."

De Hasard fortunately did not look at

Darnley's expression as he bent over his little cousin's hand and kissed the air over her palm. "But of course! How very kind of you to ask. It shall be quite like old times."

"Oh, indeed! There is so very much to talk about—so much has happened—but you must have been traveling for hours and hours, and you must be exhausted. We shall go up at once. Kirby shall ride my horse and I shall ride in your phaeton," Lydia decided, looping her arm through her cousins.

"Pity me," Mr. Darnley said in an undertone to Augusta as he turned his high-crowned beaver about in his hand.

"I think Monsieur de Hasard is quite charming," Augusta murmured in reply.

"We shall talk about all of that later," Darnley promised as he made his exit.

Brother and sister stood on the front steps and watched them riding down the lane, Lydia handling de Hasard's phaeton with exclamations of excitement, Darnley and Kirby riding behind, united for once in their obvious distaste for this charming French cousin.

"Odd sort of fellow," the major remarked, a shade of what Augusta preceived to be jealousy in his voice as brother and sister turned and walked back into the house. "Do you know, I could have sworn when I first saw him that he was the same fellow who had that overturn on the road to Hand Cross that night."

"I thought precisely the same thing,"

Augusta admitted. "But, of course, I do not think it could possibly have been him."

"Nonetheless, for once I find myself in agreement with Darnley. By Jove, did you see the look on his face? He would have just as soon strangled the fellow as look at him."

"It would appear that Mr. Darnley believes Lydia's French relations to be a most ramshackle set, you know," Augusta said shortly, looking at her hair in the mirror above the sideboard in the hall. "But I think Monsieur de Hasard is perfectly charming—and quite romantic. Why, he was smuggled out of Paris in the Terror in a cart of cabbages."

"Aye, and so was every other emigre, to hear them tell it," the major muttered darkly. Seeing that mulish look on his sister's face, he shook his head. "Well, it's not worth coming to blows about, is it? As long as Lydia's happy to see him, then I shall be happy. I wonder what's for tea? I'm as hungry as a horse!"

"Scones and macaroons, and if that is the gig with Mrs. Parrot I hear, coming back from the Larches, I very much fear chicken-foot jelly," Augusta said, examining the dregs of the teapot before ringing the bell. "Won't our Parry be sorry that she has missed it all? I daresay an afternoon in the company of Mrs. Hunt would not be half so diverting."

"I daresay an afternoon in the company of the very devil himself would be preferable to one spent with Mrs. Hunt—and all the Misses

Hunt." The major shuddered eloquently.

"I suppose we shall find out," Augusta remarked gloomily. "We are due there some night this week for a musical evening. Surely Miss Sophia will play her harp."

"I think my leg shall pain me entirely too much to move from my bed that evening," the major remarked innocently.

"I imagine we shall have to provide some sort of entertainment ourselves before too long," Augusta said, half to herself. "I wonder how long Monsieur de Hasard means to stay in the neighborhood?"

William threw his sister an odd look, but years of experience had taught him to hold the worst of his remarks to himself when she had that dreamy look upon her face.

Let Mrs. Parrot deal with it, he thought, and ate the last of the macaroons from the tea tray as Augusta rang for a fresh pot.

11

Augusta had often noticed that the perversity of her muse seemed to run hand in hand with her own ability to write herself into a corner. It had rained all that morning while she had struggled with ways and means to extricate Horrida from the clutches of Dreadnought, her amorous villain. Unfortunately, Florizel, the hero of the piece, who might have been expected to come to the rescue of his beloved, was skulking, for reasons as yet unknown, about the woods in disguise as a bandit, and was of absolutely no assistance whatsoever, being engaged in a great deal of swordplay and swashbuckling with some decidedly secondary characters. So, it would seem, it was up to the authoress to rescue Horrida, whom she disliked so thoroughly for being such a ninny as to get herself into this tangle in the first place that she was considering having her pushed from a tower window, a solution that might have satisfied Augusta but would doubtless horrify both Messieurs Clock and Fishbridge and every single one of her readers, from shopgirls to duchesses, all of whom seemed to take her work far more seriously than Miss Webb's perverse muse.

When the sun burst from behind the clouds at a few minutes past the half-hour, bathing the gray-and-green landscape with yellow sunlight and setting the sea waves to dancing with sparkling diamonds, she slid out from her desk, crept down the hall, pulled on her old cloak, and walked out the side door without so much as a twinge of guilt for her truancy.

It was an easy thing to cross the lawn and descend the stairs to the beach, where the salt wind in her hair and the spray in her face were as cleansing as a bath. Thrusting her hands into the pockets of her gray-and-white-striped gown, she bent her head against the wind and began to walk in long purposeful strides along the dreckline of the beach, stooping from time to time to pick up an interesting shell of a piece of beach glass that caught her eye. Horrida and all her woes had accompanied her like an unwanted burden, and as she walked, Augusta began to turn over and over in her mind all the possible ways in which she could write herself out of her own trap. Since these were the sort of problems she enjoyed, her spirits picked up a little, but it was not too long before the face and character of Alfred de Hasard began to intrude here and there in her meditations, and

her imagination allowed her to play—but only
a very little, for Miss Webb was not a
romantic sort of female—with a personal sort
of plot.

In this way, she walked for a mile or so,
wrapped in her own thoughts and oblivious to
anything but the cry of the gulls and the
rumble of the surf as it broke beside her feet.

"What? Out walking? I never thought that I
would see you on foot," a familiar voice said,
and startled, she looked up to see Robert
Darnley on horseback, not five feet from her,
and traveling in the opposite direction.

"You startled me," she sputtered
accusingly.

"Then I might give you a half-crown for
your thoughts," he replied, swinging down
from his mount and coming toward her, with
his crooked smile. "I was taking a shortcut to
the south downs, to see how the sheep fared.
It is easier to travel the beach than over the
guts and marshes. Out walking and thinking, I
see. Run into a snag in your novel?"

She recalled, suddenly, how he had always
been able to guess her thoughts, and pushing
a windblown strand of hair away from her
face, nodded. "I've written myself into a box
and must now write myself out of it," she
admitted as he fell into step beside her,
leading his horse.

"Perhaps if you were to tell me, I could
make a suggestion," he said. "But then again,
I have never been in the least artistic. I have

no imagination, you know, none at all."

"Oh, yes, I know that. You are everything that is prosaic," she said in a droll voice, and he nodded, laughing in agreement.

"But I am glad that I found you thus, for it saves me the trouble of having to ride over to Seaview Cottage and beg a word with you in private."

"A word in private? Whatever would we have to talk about in private?" Augusta asked naively.

Darnley threw her a look out of the corner of his eye, and the muscles in his jaw hardened slightly, but when he spoke, his tone was dispassionate. "For one thing, my ward's cousin," he said slowly. "How came he to call upon you? Did you know him when he was living in London?"

"Oh, no! Not at all. He said that he had come there first, to the cottage, because he was—because he knew you did not like him, and he was uncertain of his reception at the hall. He said you thought him the black sheep of his family. And he had a great nostalgia to see his old home again."

Darnley opened and closed his mouth, his lips setting in a thin line. He squinted over the sea into the sunlight as if making up his mind. When he spoke again, his words were measured. "I had hoped that all my troubles upon that score were dead. I was led to believe that the damned loose fish had killed himself in a carriage accident in Sea Cross," he said. "But it turned ut to be a stranger. However one could have hoped!"

"Robert," Augusta exclaimed, much shocked. "Besides, he is *not* a loose fish. He's very charming."

"I had hoped that you, of all people, would—" Darnley started to say, and then became quiet again.

She was about to tell him about the curious incident on their journey to Hand Cross from London, and the strange writing case in her possession, but unfortunately, Mr. Darnley chose that moment to express himself upon M. de Hasard.

"I suppose I have no choice but to lodge him here—he is, after all, Lydia's cousin, and for whatever reasons, she's fond of him, as was her father—but his reputation in London is not of the best, and I think it would be better if you were to set an example to the neighborhood by not receiving him. Perhaps then he'll leave all the sooner. As for me, I've no choice but to lodge him at the hall—he is family, and there'd be the devil's lot of talk if I were to turn him out, most of it coming from Lydia! She already fancies me a greater tyrant than Boney himself. But he's a slippery character, Augusta—"

"A great many of the emigres were forced to turn their hands to activities that perhaps would not have been considered genteel, but only consider that they had no choice! If he was a captain sharp, or a ladies' man or a dancing master, well, at least he was earning a living. Besides, now he has gone back to France and claimed his estates back from the Bourbons. He says he is only here to settle his business." She grew hot in de Hasard's defense. "You were always a stickler, Robert."

"I wish it were only that. I could even stand it if he'd been Greeking. But it's far worse than that—"

"You simply don't like him and you're willing to think the worst of him. I think he is very charming, and I mean to receive him as often as he wishes to come. There is nothing in my lease about whom I may and may not entertain, I might remind you."

"And I might remind you that while you think because you can write a fashionable trumpery novel, it does not precisely make you *au courant* in the ways of the real world. How like you, Augusta, to always think life is like one of your books."

"And how like you, Robert, to think that you may direct and order everyone about to suit yourself just as if we were all in your regiment! Now I recall what I most particularly disliked about you—your odious officiousness."

She suddenly found her shoulders being gripped by a pair of very strong hands, and a hungry mouth pressed against her own. Outraged, Augusta struggled, but her strength was no match for Darnley's, and after a few seconds she was not entirely certain that she would have wished it to be at that moment. Just as she ceased to struggle, he let go of her and turned away, flinging himself up on his mount.

"You must do as you wish, but, by God, Augusta, you are as bullheaded and stubborn as the general ever was. Just remember that de Hasard could never be half the man I am."

Trembling with rage and something else she would not quite define that was far more pleasurable, Augusta pulled her cloak about her shoulders and shouted to his retreating back, "You are now and you always were an odious, odious—*lout!*"

But he was well out of earshot, and the wind carried her words away toward the unlistening sea, where France was just across the water.

Augusta was still in a state of high dudgeon when she burst into the drawing room a quarter-hour later, undoing the strings of her cloak as she spoke to Mrs. Parrot, who was sitting complacently beside a warm coal fire, her hands occupied with the stitching of a tatted fringe to the edge of a cashmere shawl. "That odious, officious, tyrannical—" she began, and then, seeing that they were not alone, broke off abruptly.

M. de Hasard, elegant in pantaloons of a delicate shade of biscuit and a jacket of bottle green that needed no padding to add to his broad shoulders, was seated in the opposite chair, a glass of Madeira balanced upon his knee as if he were a member of the household. At the sight of Augusta's flushed cheeks and flashing eyes, a small, rather secretive smile crossed his handsome face, and his square jaw lifted slightly as he appraised her before rising to his feet.

"Ah, my dear Miss Webb," he said smoothly. "As you can see, I have been enjoying a most delightful cose with Mrs. Parrot. How very fortunate you are to have her companionship! We have been discussing Voltaire, and I find her ideas very stimulating."

Augusta allowed him to take her hand into his own, noting with some pleasure that he held it for a second longer than was absolutely necessary before relinquishing it with the appearance of the greatest regret for propriety.

"You have been out walking, my dear?" Mrs. Parrot said, looking at Augusta over her spectacles. "I informed Monsieur de Hasard that you frequently do so when you are stuck with a knotty problem in one of your plots."

"Yes. Down on the beach," Augusta said as she seated herself in the chair opposite de Hasard, warming her hands by the fire.

The French gentleman placed the tips of his fingers together. "While I do not claim to be a great creative mind," he said softly, "I fancy that my mind is such that I might be able to offer a humble suggestion or two, if you would but tell me about your work."

Augusta looked doubtful, but very soon explained the knot into which she had allowed her characters to become tangled.

De Hasard pursed his lips, playing with the ends of his elaborate cravat and closing his eyes, while Mrs. Parrot and Miss Webb watched him with the same interest they might have accorded a magician about to produce a scarf from a hat.

"If I were you," M. de Hasard said at last, "and I would never claim just such a genius, I would simply manifest an apparition that would affright this villain so very much that he would have no choice but to relinquish his grip upon your poor Horrida, fall into a swoon, and allow her time to escape. Murdered wives are always an excellent choice for a ghost, you know."

Augusta sat with her mouth quite slack for several seconds. Then she clapped her hands together. "Precisely! How wonderful you are! Why did I not think of that? It is exactly the way out of the problem—and then the ghost may unlock the tower door and allow Horrida to escape to the forest, where she will of course find that stupid Florizel." She gazed upon M. de Hasard with warm eyes. "How can I ever thank you?" she asked warmly.

He bowed graciously. "By allowing me to have the waltz with you at Mrs. Hunt's this week. Please say you will be there. It is the only thing that will make the Larches bearable to me."

"Of course I shall be there! We cannot very well go to Mrs. Leigh's and not appear at Mrs. Hunt's," Augusta exclaimed.

"Two very droll ladies," M. de Hasard promised, rolling his eyes heavenward. "However, one should see old friends. Tell me, how do the Misses Hunt do? Has she fired Sophie off?"

"Only one Season, and she did not take," Augusta said. "I believe she had high hopes for my brother, but he has fixed his interest on Lydia."

"So I have noticed," de Hasard said. "This morning I noticed, as I was driving in, the pair of them on horseback, riding across the downs, with that dreary groom of my cousin's trailing behind. Poor man, he never did approve of me, any more than Mr. Darnley. In *that*, at least, they are united."

"You must stay to lunch, *monsieur*," Mrs. Parrot said, looking at the clock on the mantel. "And tell us all about Paris. How well I recall visiting there when the general was alive, in '03. Such a lovely city."

"Ah, but you must see the Hotel Hasard, my house on the Rue Brinviellers. It was built by Le Brun for my great-great-grandfather as his town house in Paris, when he was living at Versailles. Of course, during the Directoire, some really unspeakable people occupied it and ruined the tapestries and the silver furniture, but we fared a little better with Bonaparte . . ." His voice trailed away as he rose to follow the ladies to the morning room, where Crockett had laid out their luncheon. "But what tragedy, what history . . . our estates in the Loire."

For the remainder of the afternoon, he entertained them with his family history, striking exactly the correct blend of irony and pride that was bound to appeal to two ladies of somewhat less grand origins and ancestry and romantic notions.

When he left, Augusta, still smarting beneath the events of her encounter with Darnley that morning, encouraged him to visit them as often as he liked, and as soon as she was alone with Mrs. Parrot, she pronounced him a most fascinating man.

"Yes," Mrs. Parrot said slowly, "he is indeed very charming." But her tone was not one of great enthusiasm, and Augusta a little piqued that her beloved Parry did not share her admiration for the handsome Frenchman, decided not to relate the encounter with Robert Darnley to her preceptress.

12

If Mrs. Parrot was reserved in her opinion of M. de Hasard, it was only in contrast to Augusta and Lydia, both of whom, in their own ways, positively doted upon him. Indeed, so much was he to be found in their company that William, upon coming on him seated in his favorite chair in the drawing room one day, limped away again, mumbling beneath his breath, "Does that damned fop live here?"

It might have been small comfort to him that his opinion was shared by both Mr. Darnley and John Kirby, but it did serve to draw the three of them together in a male preserve in which M. de Hasard could not attempt to join, as he was fond neither of sailing nor of horseback riding nor of agriculture, which had become, in the absence of the ladies, the chief pre-occupations shared by these three males.

Of Mr. Darnley, Augusta was happy to see very little; she still smarted from their encounter on the beach and preferred to avoid him as much as possible. Nor did she miss his company, for M. de Hasard filled her days and evenings very admirably, thank you.

He never seemed to lose interest in the smallest details of her work and indeed was able to read aloud from her books with such feeling that, as Lydia declared, "It was like to make your bones shake." He played the violin and accompanied Lydia when she sang, and was happy to turn the pages of her music whenever Augusta played at the pianoforte; he was also more than willing to teach them both the latest steps of the new polonaise, the dance that was sweeping Paris. He seemed to know everyone and everything, and his gossip was delicious, spiced as it was with just the right combination of truth and malice. No one could have been more *au courant* with the latest fashions, and he was willing to spend hours with Augusta, pouring over the latest issues of *La Belle Assemblee*, while his tales of Paris life were enticing.

"Man-milliner," sniffed Miss Polestack, and was roundly snubbed by Augusta for her observation.

Nor was he ignored by Mrs. Leigh and Mrs. Hunt, whose rivalry went into a frenzy in their attempt to entertain with so many interesting guests in their midsts.

Indeed, Mrs. Hunt had just left, after inviting them all to a musicale at her house in a fortnight's time, when M. de Hasard made his suggestion.

"My dear Miss Webb," he drawled, lounging among the cushions on the sofa, "poor Lydia, not yet being out, cannot entertain, of course, at the hall, but you could certainly have a most amusing little party here." He smiled his toothy smile at her, drawing his hand across the back of the couch.

"A party? Here?" Augusta asked blankly.

"Well, my dear, you cannot expect everyone else to entertain you and not at least give them one chance to see the inside of your house, can you?" Alfred asked reasonably.

Augusta glanced at Mrs. Parrot to see how she was taking this. "We do owe, my dear, Mrs. Hunt, Mrs. Leigh, the vicar and Mrs. Simpson, the Otwells—we have even dined once or twice with Robert and Lydia, without ever really providing them with a formal reciprocation."

"I hardly thought we were on terms of formality with them."

"That may be. But, my dear, the point is that Monsieur de Hasard is quite correct; it behooves us to think about getting up an entertainment for our neighbors here."

"Perhaps we should have a ball?" Augusta asked, only a little sarcastically.

De Hasard winced. "But where would you dance? There is no ballroom at the cottage, a sad lack that I always deplored when I lived here."

"You might use the one at the hall," Lydia said. She had been listening to this conversation with great interest.

"Oh, my dear cousin, you know depressing

old Robert would never agree to that," de Hasard said. "So, I fear, dancing is out of the question. Only think how very tiresome it is at Mrs. Hunt's, when more than four or five couples attempt to dance in that little music room, everyone bumping and banging into one another. Quite depressing! The other night I almost tripped over poor Sophie Hunt and that spotty Burton boy."

"Jack, and he would be very angry if he heard you describe him so." Lydia giggled. "Whenever I am around you, all my friends have always seemed like such children, Alfred."

"But since I could give you at least sixteen years, cousin, that is only to be expected," M. de Hasard pointed out reasonably. "You must recall that I am centuries older than you and your friends."

Lydia sighed, propping her chin in her hand. It was to be noted that her manners, under the tutelage of Mrs. Parrot, had taken a turn for the better lately. At least she was not lounging all over her chair, with one leg thrown over the arm, but was seated in a passably decorous manner, with her ankles neatly crossed.

"But how shall I entertain?" Augusta asked, bringing the subject around again to the point that interested her.

"Ah, yes, what, what, what shall we do?" de Hasard asked, leaning back and closing his eyes, as if waiting for inspiration.

"Nothing on a London scale, mind you," Augusta warned. "This house simply isn't big enough for that."

"But, my dear lady, everyone will expect something original from you, you know. You are, after all, a well-known artiste."

"You make me sound like an opera dancer."

"Well, not quite that bad, I should hope. A literary artiste, of course." De Hasard laughed.

"Well, a ball is out of the question, and so is a musicale—that is Mrs. Hunt's province, just as the dinner party is Mrs. Leigh's," Augusta mused thoughtfully.

"A costume party?" Lydia suggested.

"A famous idea, dear cousin, but since we must squeeze our gala in between the entertainments of Mrs. Hunt and Mrs. Leigh, on such short notice, totally unfair. After all, not everyone has a trunk of ancestral clothes in the attic to draw from," de Hasard admonished. "Unfair, cousin!"

"Then what do you suggest, Alfred?" Augusta asked, looking at him from beneath her lashes.

"I thought, dear lady, that you would never ask," he said happily. "The answer is quite simple and quite original: al fresco!"

"Isn't he that awful Spanish bandit that William keeps talking about?" Lydia asked. "The one who—"

"No, no, you silly!" M. de Hasard sighed, rolling his eyes. "Al fresco means out-of-doors. A party out-of-doors. On the lawn and the beach, surrounded by the beauties of nature."

"Ugh," Augusta said. "The beauties of nature are lost upon me, thank you."

"What if it rains?" Lydia pointed out quite sensibly.

"It would never dare," de Hasard promised.

Looking at him, Augusta was inclined to believe it would not, simply because Alfred was that kind of a person. If he planned a party out-of-doors, it would be sunny and clement.

"I think we shall invite only about forty persons, and the festivities shall commence at noon," he was saying, holding even Mrs. Parrot captivated by his spell, woven about the room with the magic of charm. "Lydia, can one still hire that amusing band from Rye that used to come and play when your papa had the Regent to stay?"

"Oh, yes! And we can dance on the grass, you know—no lack of space on the lawn."

"Pink tents, of course. Dear me, I shall have to speak to the good Crockett. Will he enter into our schemes with pleasure, Augusta? One quite hates to see the staff going about with long faces. It is more than one can bear, you know; just seeing that lugubrious Polestack quite casts one down."

"I think Crockett is dying of boredom and would be thrilled with something to do to occupy himself," Augusta said. "He is a London man, and used to a busier life."

"Well, we shall certainly keep him busy, then," de Hasard promised. "Can we borrow staff from you, Lydia?"

"Of course. This is the most exciting thing that has happened in ages," Lydia replied, her eyes flashing.

"Very good! Now, as to food, I think we shall, of course, have a champagne punch. So fortuitous, you know, that the gardens will be at the height of their bloom when the guests arrive. Those lovely, lovely herbaceous borders . . . so grateful that Capability Brown's work extended to the landscaping of the cottage, is one not?" He was thinking aloud, with great rapidity. "Also so tragic that the English are such drudges when it comes to food. Everything boiled and bland, without a trace of imagination. Your chef, however, Augusta, is French, I believe?"

"Oh, yes, and hideously overpaid. He did not at all want to come into the country, so Mrs. Parrot had to promise him a huge bonus."

"Very well, he shall earn his wages. I shall go and speak to him myself, *en francais*, and I am certain that we will have an understanding. I think perhaps seafood, little bits of lobster and crab pastry that can be eaten from a tiny little Limoges plate . . . The Limoges service is still at the hall, is it not? Good! Tarts of fruit and chocolate and spun sugar; curried sole . . . Heavens, one's mouth waters just thinking about it! It is precisely what one would do, you know, at Hotel de

Hasard, when Antoinette was still alive, poor dear thing. If only one could dress you all up as shepherdesses of the *ancien regime*, but no," he sighed regretfully, "I suppose that is going too far."

"Indeed," Mrs. Parrot sniffed.

"Yes, I suppose so," M. de Hasard agreed regretfully. But his spirits were depressed only for a moment before he brightened up again. "Now, my dear Augusta, you must get your writing paper and we shall spend the rest of the afternoon writing out invitations for all our guests," he commanded. "Leave everything to me; I promise you shall have a most amusing party. The best party ever!"

Obediently, Augusta did as she was told.

Surprisingly, Mr. Darnley's reaction to the news was mild. When he came to fetch Lydia away, he merely raised an eyebrow. "We have become quite social here," he said casually. "I fear when you leave us, the countryside will be very dull indeed."

Augusta, standing in the hallway to bid Lydia good-bye, frowned slightly. She had not thought that she would have to leave eventually, nor that Darnley would be one of the persons she would have to leave behind her. She was surprised at her own reaction and sought to cover it with a little laugh. "Well, at least we are not dull," she promised.

"No, but it would seem that Lydia ought to have a new dress and some sort of frippery for the event," Mr. Darnley said, turning his high-crowned beaver about in his hands.

Lydia was instantly alight with happiness. "Oh, Robert, might I?" she exclaimed, and impulsively hugged him.

"Here, now! People will get the idea that we actually deal well together if you don't stop that," Mr. Darnley exclaimed with a smile. "Augusta, could you—would you be kind enough to take her into Rye and see that she has what she needs? I'll stand the bills, of course. I think the estate can stand the expense of a new gown for Lady Towson."

"What's this about the estate?" the major asked, coming into the hallway. "Hello, Lydia, Goose. Darnley's been taking me about the farms and the wolds. Never knew there was so much to learn about handling land and crops before."

"We might make a farmer of him yet," Mr. Darnley said to Augusta with a tiny wink. "Should tomorrow be too late for you? I can send Lydia about in the phaeton in the morning, if it's convenient for you."

Lydia looked so hopeful that Augusta did not have the heart to plead her work as a priority. "Of course," she agreed.

Shortly after breakfast the next morning, Darnley's phaeton, with Lydia driving and John Kirby standing up behind, pulled up to the portico of the cottage, and Augusta climbed in and was driven away.

Lydia was more voluble than ever, excited

at the prospect of a trip to Rye and the purchase of a new gown, so that all that was required of Augusta was an occasional "Oh, really?" or "You don't say!" as they whipped along the lanes toward Sea Cross and the Rye Road. Darnley obviously had no worries about lending his vehicle to his young cousin: like all the Towsons, Lydia was a superb horsewoman, and handled the precarious phaeton with a great deal of skill.

"Oh," she said when Augusta complimented her. "When I was six, Papa put me up on the perch and made me drive through a narrow gatepost until I could do so without scratching the paint. Hullo, what's that at the doctor's house? It looks like Alfred's rig."

They pulled up before a narrow brick house, set away from the rest of Sea Cross by a high hedge, and Lydia leaned across Augusta to call down to a serious-looking older man in the dark clothes of the medical profession. "Good morning, Dr. Newcomb! What is my cousin doing at your house? Is he sick?"

The doctor, who had obviously known Lady Towson all her life, strolled over to take her hand and shake his gray head, frowning. "No, he's come to make the arrangements to ship that Lamballe fellow back to France. Died during the night, you know—or you soon will, for I'm sure it's all over the village." He removed his spectacles and began to polish them on the tail of his coat.

"What, Georges Lamballe, dead?" Lydia exclaimed. "But I thought he was doing so well."

"He was, for a while, then he took a turn for the worse. Brain fever," the doctor remarked, shaking his head. "This is what comes of galloping about the countryside in those dashed fancy phaetons! They're no safe vehicle for anyone, particularly one so wreckless in his ways as Lamballe was! Well, I did what I could, but in the end it was no good, and now he'll go back to his family in a butt of whiskey, like the Duke of Clarence, say, what?"

At that moment, Alfred de Hasard appeared from the house, looking very grave. When he saw the two ladies in the phaeton, Augusta thought a distinct look of annoyance passed over his expression, but he quickly concealed it as he stepped forward to greet them.

"It is too, too tragic," he sighed. "Poor Georges has died. I am devastated, but what can one do? He would drink, and he would try to come down here to find me, and you see how it all happens."

Augusta thought she heard Kirby snort, up behind them on his perch, but she was not certain.

"Please," de Hasard implored them, "drive on! In a very short time the undertakers will be here, and I would not wish you to be thrown into the mopes."

"As if one would, about Georges Lamballe,"

Lydia remarked after they had said their fare-
wells and driven away. "He was a thoroughly
bad sort, you know. Even Papa said so! But
one cannot help but wonder what he was
doing down here...." She shrugged and
turned the talk toward fashions.

It was as Alfred de Hasard predicted, and
the day fixed for the al-fresco party dawned
bright and sunny, as sunny as de Hasard's
mood. If he had been at all cast down by the
demise of his friend, the mysterious M. Lamballe, he seemed not to show it in the days
that followed, as he busily planned every
detail of Augusta's party.

Whenever Augusta expressed doubt that
such an elaborate affair as M. de Hasard
envisioned could possibly be brought off
within such a short space of time, he merely
tut-tutted her and advised her to attend to her
toilette for the event, for he promised that she
would shine as a hostess.

However, on the appointed day, she
awakened to find a pink-and-white-striped
silk tent going up on the lawn, and a small if
determined army of carpenters, caterers,
vintners, florists, and musicians all moving
like so many ants about their preordained
business, transforming the sweeping lawn
into a playground for forty selected guests,
with M. de Hasard, apparently in his element,
directing it all like the conductor of an
orchestra.

"Well," sniffed Polestack as she laid out Augusta's gown for the event, "I never thought that Frenchman could do it, but he has, miss, and that's a fact, although what decent Christian people should want to do with eating and drinking and dancing out of doors, when there's a perfectly good house to do it all in, I do not know."

Polestack's opinions aside, when Augusta descended the stairs a few minutes to noon, she already knew that the al fresco would be a success, for carriages were already rolling up the drive.

"But, my dear, how ravishing you are," de Hasard exclaimed, advancing upon her and holding out both his hands to take her own.

And indeed, Augusta was feeling at her best. She wore a lawn day dress trimmed in Brussels lace about the bishop sleeves and high, ruffled neck. A belt of pink satin, embroidered with roses and Michaelmas daisies, was gathered beneath the slightly dropped waist, and the bonded hem was runched with tiny roses and daisies in the same hues. Upon her feet she wore rose satin slippers, and over her curls she had tied a straw leghorn hat, trimmed with ribbon and roses, and she carried an organdy parasol.

"Perfect, perfect," de Hasard enthused, kissing her hands. "Now you must come and greet your guests."

Augusta walked out on the terrace and surveyed the scene. All was in readiness. Beneath the pink tent, the food, a veritable feast of her chef's art, was spread out for display, almost too beautiful to eat, while a waiter was uncorking the first bottle of champagne. Just as Lydia and Darnley, accompanied by the major, came around the corner, the band began to play.

"Oh, Lydia," Augusta sighed, filled with pleasure.

"Isn't she smashing?" the major asked fondly.

"She is indeed," Mr. Darnley agreed, "thanks to you, Augusta."

And Lydia was looking lovely indeed. Gazing at her fondly, Augusta was certain that no other female at the party would be quite so beautiful. There was just a thread of self-consciousness in the way she turned about, so that Augusta could see her toilette, but it enhanced rather than detracted from her charm.

Her dressmaker in Rye had worked to Augusta's specifications for the gown featured in the latest edition of *La Belle Assemblée* to produce the confection that now adorned the young Lady Towson, and the effect was stunning.

A pale-blue printed muslin had been worked into a thousand tiny pleats that radiated from a low neckline and flowed into the slashed and faggoted sleeves, turned in blue lawn and trimmed with ivory ribbon. From the body of the dress, the tiny pleats dropped to the hem, richly trimmed with rosettes of blue silk and tiers of point-de-Venise lace. It was the perfect gown for a girl just on the verge of her debut, and the chip-straw hat, fastened beneath her chin with ivory satin ribbon, and the ivory slippers upon her feet set it off to perfection.

As her eyes met Augusta's, she smiled, and would not have been Lydia if one long-lash-fringed lid did not drop in a wink.

"There you are," Augusta said. "Now go and have a glass of champagne. Only one, mind, and then you may have orgeat," she added as Lydia and the major moved off.

More guests were arriving, Mr. and Mrs. Leigh and the vicar and his wife all agog at the pink tent and the band, with the poor, bracket-faced Hunt sisters right behind.

"I would say more, but you must greet your guests now," Darnley said in a low voice to her. "Perhaps we might have a dance in the grass later?"

Before her reply could form on her lips, he had moved away, and she had no more time to consider his meaning, for her attentions were claimed by the receiving line.

"Everyone is having such a good time," de Hasard said to her as he walked by with the dowager Lady Cunningby on his arm, and indeed, it would seem that they were.

The sun beamed down upon a happy scene as people helped themselves to plates of food and glasses of champagne, and settled in, right upon the grass, to converse and listen to the music of the band, enjoying the beauty of the day and the view of the sea.

Augusta was amused to see Mrs. Leigh, all in lace and ruffles, settling down very easily in the shade of the chestnut trees, her plate heaped with delicious goodies, de Hasard propping her back with a cushion.

"Such a novel idea, Miss Webb," the vicar's wife said as she went back to the tent for a second helping of trifle. "The vicar is ever so much pleased."

"It was all Monsieur de Hasard's doing," Augusta said.

She was about to go in search of Mrs. Parrot when a hand was slipped beneath her elbow, and she turned to see Robert Darnley grinning down at her.

"I thought I should claim my dance now, before de Hasard whisks you away," he said with his sardonic grin. "Save I am afraid that you will put my eye out with that parasol of yours."

As she put her sunshade down, Augusta laughed. "If anyone whisks me away, it is liable to be Mrs. Parrot, reminding me that the duchess claims my attention. How very civil I have been today!"

"Quite unlike you, you know. I expect you would prefer to see us all at perdition, and your writing before you."

"Actually, I would prefer a plate of food. I have not had as much as a glass of champagne today and only tea and toast for breakfast. Feed me, and then I will dance with you, I promise."

"Your wish must be my command," Darnley said, and Augusta frowned slightly. Noticing, he looked at her quizzically. "Have I said something wrong, then?" he asked.

She shook her head. "No, it is only that that was what you used to say to me, at those garrison dances, so long ago . . ."

"Yes, I suppose I did. Old habits die hard. Forgive me if it caused a goose to run over your grave. Champagne . . ." He took two glasses from a passing waiter and led her toward the tent, where he proceeded to fill a plate with a great deal of food. "But we were not talking about the past—we were talking about your writing. How goes it?"

"As always, in fits and starts. Oh, I would very much like some cold ham, please."

"You know, when your first book came out, I could hardly believe that you were the author."

"You did not think I could write?" Augusta asked as they walked across the lawn toward a place where several ancient boxwoods sheltered a bench.

"Oh, no, I never doubted that you could write. I only doubted my senses, for what you write about is so macabre."

"Not at all like me?"

"Not as I knew you."

"I don't know how to explain it, save that

one day I was reading a novel and I tossed it aside and said, 'Well! *I* can do better than that!' or some such silly thing, and I sat down and I like to think that I *did* do better than that.'' She sat down on the bench and addressed her plate with good appetite.

"There can be no question about that, of course,'' Darnley said, sipping his champagne.

"And what have you been doing for the past ten years?'' Augusta asked conversationally.

Darnley shrugged his shoulders. "Well, after I left Niepert, I was posted to Vienna for a while, then home to London.''

"London? What did you do in London?''

"Oh, a little of this and a little of that. Whatever needed to be done,'' Darnley said vaguely. "Nothing terribly interesting. Vienna was much better. Lots of pretty females there.''

"So I understand. The Congress must have been quite exciting.''

"It was interesting. I learned to waltz very well.''

"Then I shall expect you to waltz me about on the grass, if you please, just as soon as I am finished with eating.''

"Then you must finish at once, Augusta, for they are playing a waltz I was particularly fond of in Vienna, and I see several couples are already on the floor, as it were.''

"Mmm—'' Augusta said, but she was ruthlessly placed upon her feet and led to the open space before the terrace, where several other couples were happily twirling about in time to the strains of the music played by the band.

Darnley smiled down upon Augusta diabolically. "Now, my little scrivener, we shall see how well you and I play on a grass court."

"Robert!" Augusta laughed, half-protesting, but only half, for she was soon caught up in the music and the motion, and closed her eyes, humming the tune beneath her breath as Darnley moved her about the grass in his masterful fashion.

"There," he said, so low that only she could hear him. "Some things are never forgotten, as you can see, Augusta."

"No," she had to agree in a small, breathless voice. She wanted the moment to go on forever, for she loved dancing with him, and always had. And perhaps always would, she thought, before reminding herself that she intended to lead the life of a maiden lady, forever and ever.

The feel of his hand against her waist, the way in which he spun her about the floor—these were the things that nothing could obliterate from her memory.

All too suddenly, the dance was over and she felt as if she were awakening from a dream, an automaton applauding politely, a dreamer among the awake. She turned, looking up at Darnley, but he was frowning, and she followed his stare to see Alfred de Hasard crossing the lawn toward them.

"I believe I may claim the next dance?" he said smoothly, taking Augusta's arm in his own.

Darnley bowed sardonically. "Just as you say," he murmured, and Augusta watched him walk away, around the corner of the house.

"Well, my dear Augusta," de Hasard said, "shall we dance?"

13

"I fear," Mrs. Hunt of the Larches was saying, "that my poor musicale will be quite cast in the shade by your lovely al fresco of last week, but I also hope that I may still count upon you to attend."

Augusta, who had been staring out the window at the rain and wondering why she had not seen Darnley since the day of her party, forced herself to pay attention to her visitor. "Heavens, ma'am, of course we shall," she promised. "Although we have all grown quite grand, what with so many suppers and country dances and assemblies and routs."

"Nothing as vulgar, mind you as one of the shows put on by Mrs. Leigh—heavens, she could entertain in Astley's Ampitheatre—but only an evening of the most exclusive persons in the region of the most refined sensibilities, of course," Mrs. Hunt promised.

"Is Mrs. Leigh coming?" Augusta had been unable to resist asking.

"Oh, heavens yes, if only to allow her to see how things are properly done," Mrs. Hunt had assured her.

She was, therefore, totally unsurprised when her brother begged off, saying that he and Darnley preferred to attend a boxing match being held in Rye. If she had not felt so out of sorts with the major at that point, she would well have expressed her own fervent wish to be able to go to anything, even something so horrid as an exhibition of fisticuffs btween Gentleman Jackson and the West Indian Black, for she could think of nothing that appealed to her less than an evening spent listening to the decidedly amateur musical efforts of the Hunt sisters and the curate.

Mrs. Parrot, who was far too well-bred to express any sentiments about the evening's plans whatsoever, merely looked up at the major over her glasses. "Do dress warmly, my dear William," she advised, "and be certain to do just as Robert asks, since you will be his guest tonight."

"If you think that means we're all going to get foxed, have no fear," the major answered cheerfully. "We're taking the curricle and Kirby is driving us. I think he has a fancy to see the match too."

"Odious," Augusta muttered when her brother went off whistling cheerfully. "At least you notice that Monsieur de Hasard has not deserted us."

"No, I see that he has not," Mrs. Parrot said, looking up at the clock on the mantelpiece. "And speaking of which, if we are to dine with

Lydia and Monsieur de Hasard tonight, I think we should think about dressing now."

It was with no very great expectations that Augusta, in company with Mrs. Parrot, arrived at the hall, and was shown to the green salon, where their hostess was waiting.

For a moment, as they were announced, it seemed to Augusta that both de Hasard and Lydia were flushed, and she was not entirely certain she had not seen them drawing apart, as if they had been interrupted in an embrace.

But the way in which Lydia moved forward to greet her, her face flushed with excitement and her manner lively, might have been cause for some suspicion had not de Hasard, when Lady Towson was talking to Mrs. Parrot in her swift and animated voice, seized the opportunity to take Augusta's hand into his own and gaze soulfully into her eyes.

"How very charming you are looking tonight," he said. "I believe that blue is your best color. How much I should yearn to see you in that gown, moving through Hotel de Hasard in Paris, the envy of all."

Augusta smiled with pleasure, knowing that she was looking her best in a dinner gown of celestial-blue crepe, cut low in the bosom and trimmed with runchings of ivory and rose silk. Polestack had dressed her hair a la Athene, and she carried a spangled shawl of silver gauze over her shoulders.

"And you, too, look very handsome in your evening clothes," she told de Hasard, in

admiration of his teal coat and *corbeau-*
colored breeches, his cravat tied in the style
known as the *trone d'amour*, his chestnut
locks pomaded and brushed a la Brutus.

"All for you," he murmured with a little
smile. "Certainly not for the Hunt sisters. Do
you think that the very spotty one will play
that dreadful Scotch ballad again tonight? It
makes me wince."

"Then you will be in agony when Miss
Marantha Hunt favors us with a rendition of
her French love ballads," Augusta promised.

He sighed and shook his head, going to bend
over Mrs. Parrot's hand while Lydia, eyes
dancing, approached Augusta.

"You are looking very much the lady
tonight," she said approvingly, noting young
Lady Towson's gown of pale-rose-striped
sateen. "That gown is most becoming, my
dear."

"Do you think so?" Lydia asked. "Alfred
picked it out from an *Ackerman's* at my
dressmaker's. How wonderful it will be
tonight, to be among friends and laugh at the
Hunts, although one should really not, I
know. But without Robert to frown me down,
I feel positively free."

"And what about poor William?" Augusta
asked.

Lydia thrust out her lower lip. "If he would
prefer to see a pair of grown men engage in
fisticuffs with each other than be with me,
that is *his* loss, and so I told him!" She

grinned roguishly. "Anyway, in a day or two I shall forgive him and then all will be well again."

Augusta linked her arm comfortably into her friend's. "I begin to think you understand my brother very well." She laughed.

After dinner, the carriage was called for and they proceeded the few miles to the Larches beneath a cloudy sky that threatened rain.

"I am glad that we ate a large meal, for we will get nothing from the Hunts," Lydia promised them, and Augusta saw that it was true.

In contrast to the studied opulence of the Grange, the Larches was a stark Queen Anne box of red brick, as emptily landscaped with low, scraggly shrubs as it was sparsely furnished inside.

A half-starved-looking maid answered the door and they were relieved of their cloaks and shown to the music room, where perhaps ten gloomy-looking persons, including a number of Hunt sisters, sat about in uncomfortable attitudes.

Mrs. Hunt herself made to greet them, wearing a dun-colored gown that had certainly seen better days and done better things. Mr. Hunt, as skeletal and dark-clad as his wife, was by her side.

"Every time I come here," Mrs. Leigh said as she bustled up to them, covered tonight in feathers, "I wonder where I ought to look for the coffin. Did you note the refreshment table? A wheel of cheese and six lobster patties for twelve. Shabby is what I call it!"

Clearly disappointed that she would have to make do with two fewer eligible bachelors than she had counted upon Mrs. Hunt drifted off with M. de Hasard in tow, hoping to interest him in the dubious charms of her second daughter, Marantha; apparently she had given up all hope for Sophia.

The evening was interminable for Augusta, who had a good ear for music and box seats at the Philharmonic Hall and the Opera, consisting as it did of a series of recitals by the Hunt daughters, who to a female were pathetically untalented, in spite of all their mother's ambitions for their accomplishments.

It seemed to her that it was almost a blessing when a sudden clap of thunder, followed by a great flash of lightning, drowned out Miss Susan Hunt's whining rendition of a plaintive English ballad. Clap after clap of thunder followed, accompanied by great bursts of lightning that threw the room into sharp illumination.

More than one guest was happy to seize upon the excuse of the torrential rainfall as a means of making an early exit, and Augusta and Lydia were among the first to rise from the chairs.

"Saved by an act of merciful Providence!" Lydia laughed as the old coach plunged through the mud. "Next Sunday I shall be particularly attentive when the vicar reads the blessing."

If Mrs. Parrot thought young Lady Towson indulging in impiety, she said nothing, but her look was enough to cause Lydia to cast down her eyes.

"I for one have always believed that the Lord is a gentleman of taste," M. de Hasard announced.

The coach rumbled up before the portals of the cottage and the younger ladies bid each other a laughing good night, promising to meet again very soon.

As the footman opened the door, M. de Hasard gallantly jumped down. "Allow me . . ." he began, and then, to the horror of those watching him, he slipped on the wet stone steps and landed at a very odd angle, upon his back.

"Are you all right?" Augusta asked, standing in the door of the carriage while the horrified footman, uncertain what to do, looked on.

"F-forgive me, but I think I have wrenched my back. I cannot get up," M. de Hasard said with a pained and apologetic smile.

14

The scene might have come from one of her novels, Augusta thought: three women in evening dress, standing about a prone man, while rain poured down upon them all.

"So very clumsy of me," M. de Hasard sighed, looking very pale indeed in the light thrown over the scene by a very rattled and suddenly aged-looking Crockett. "I misjudged the step and took"—he winced eloquently—"a fall. Do forgive me."

"But you must forgive *us*," Augusta said, dabbing at the rain falling upon his head with her handkerchief, an inadequate bit of linen and lace.

"Oh, Cousin Alfred, are you in a great deal of pain?" Lydia asked anxiously, flittering about in a state of nerves.

"Crockett, hand Miss Augusta the lantern and bring an umbrella at once. And you might as well send a couple of footmen also," Mrs. Parrot said evenly. "We shall have to move Monsieur de Hasard inside, since it is fairly ridiculous for all of us to be standing here in the rain doing nothing."

"So kind, so dependable," M. de Hasard said, turning his white face toward Mrs. Parrot. "I knew, madam, that you would know precisely what to do."

"Well, I do not, and that's a fact, until I can see what you have injured, but if you will endure but a little longer, I hope that we shall endeavor to make you a little more comfortable."

With the aid of Lydia's coachman, the footman carried de Hasard into the house and laid him on the couch in the drawing room, while Lydia called for hartshorn and burnt feathers.

"No, no," de Hasard said, waving her away. "It is my back, cousin."

"Should we send for the doctor?" Augusta asked Mrs. Parrot.

"Oh, no, no, no, please," de Hasard said swiftly. "No doctors, please, I beg of you! It is an old injury only, and one I have had before. A wrench of the muscles, that is all. A few day's bed rest, and all shall be well."

"Then I think we ought to put Monsieur de Hasard to bed here, rather than allow him to jounce and bounce in the coach toward the hall," Augusta suggested.

"Oh, no, I do not mean to cause any trouble," de Hasard sighed, wincing as a spasm passed over him.

"Nonsense!" Augusta said firmly. "It will be no trouble at all, I promise you. Crockett, will you see that the red chamber is made up for Monsieur de Hasard."

The Frenchman gripped her arm so tightly that it hurt. His smile was that of a skull. "Please, if you please, dear lady—the bed-chamber you now occupy was mine when I was a child. I think I could rest comfortably upon that mattress."

"Of course, of course, whatever you want shall be seen to," Augusta promised. "Crockett, will you ask Polestack to make the necessary arrangements? I shall sleep in the red chamber tonight, and Monsieur de Hasard shall occupy my own."

"Very good, Miss Augusta," said Crockett in a tone that implied it was not very good at all, as far as he was concerned, and turned, with a speaking glance at Miss Polestack, lingering in the doorway, to obey her commands.

"I think that what will make you feel very much more the thing," Mrs. Parrot said calmly, "is a little restorative, you know."

"Some brandy would be very nice," de Hasard said faintly.

"Oh, no, my good *monsieur*, I was thinking more of a remedy of my own devising: elder-berry wine with a little chicken-foot jelly." With a stately tread, she went off to the kitchen to prepare this sovereign remedy.

"Truly, only a little brandy—" de Hasard murmured.

"Now, Cousin Alfred, you must listen to Mrs. Parrot. She knows everything," Lydia exclaimed, perching on the edge of the couch.

The gentleman closed his eyes. "Lydia," he

said at last, "I think perhaps you ought to go home. It is enough that one of us is here to put these good people out . . ."

Lydia, who had looked a trifle bored, now that the excitement was over, nodded as she saw the assent in Augusta's eyes. "I cannot keep the coachman waiting," she said. "It is already past his bedtime." She picked up her wrap from the chair and kissed Augusta on the cheek. "Should you need anything during the night from the hall, you have only to send up for it."

"My nightdress, my shaving things, my robe, my—" M. de Hasard said faintly, one hand gesturing lazily in the air.

Lady Towson looked at Miss Webb, smiling dimly, as if to say, "Men!" However, she merely pecked at Augusta's cheek, remarking aloud, "I shall go and say good night to Mrs. Parrot and be upon my way. Trust me to come as soon as you need me."

"I shall, but I doubt it will be necessary, so pray do not worry," Augusta advised her.

Since Lady Towson had never in her life been known to worry about anything, she merely laughed a silvery tinkle as she went out the door.

"I think we had best get you into bed where you can rest," Augusta told M. de Hasard after Lydia had exited the room.

"Yes," he said faintly, "that would be very nice."

Leaving him in the hands of Crockett, who

was busily directing two footmen toward the paneled chamber, Augusta, utterly exhausted, collapsed into a chair beside the fire and, in a most unladylike manner, put her feet up on the grate, fanning herself with the unburnt feathers Crockett had brought up from the kitchen.

It was all very well to have M. de Hasard as a visitor, she thought, but to have him as a houseguest for an indefinite period of time was far more than she had bargained for. She was a little surprised at her own flash of annoyance, and more than a little plagued with guilt as she comtemplated, with the most severe dismay, the ruined condition of her once lovely celestial-blue gown.

"And I still owe Madame Elvira four hundred pounds for this," she wailed aloud, fingering the places in the hem where the pink silk roses had run purple streaks into the ivory runching. Not even Polestack's genius would ever be able to restore *this*, she thought. She was just about to castigate herself for worrying about such trivialities while a man lay injured upstairs when the door to the drawing room opened a crack and Robert Darnley thrust his head through the opening.

His hair was plastered to his skull with rainwater, and his shirt points had long ago wilted. As he peered at Augusta, she noted that he was swaying a little unsteadily on his feet, and a most ridiculous grin was fixed to his features.

"Is it safe?" the major asked, peering over

his shoulder, in very much the same condition. "They all gone to bed—hic—?"

Mr. Darnley shook his head from side to side. "No, young fool. Can you see your sister sitting right there beside the fire, lookin' very much like a drowned rat." He broke into giggles at his own joke, and Augusta tried to muster what dignity she could by staring down her decidedly too-short-for-staring-down nose at them.

"You are both drunk," she hissed indignantly.

"And you look as if you've been rollin' in the mud, Goose," the major said, pushing Darnley into the room before him. "So don't rag *our* heads off."

"As if I would," Augusta said with whatever dignity she could muster, watching as they headed for the brandy cabinet and helped themselves most generously, giggling like a pair of schoolboys.

"What a feint!" the major said. "First a left, then a right, and then an uppercut to the jaw—"

"No, no, no, old boy! First a right, then a left, then a smashing good right hook. The Black took the Gentleman out in twenty rounds, bang!" He attempted to demonstrate, spilling brandy all over the carpet.

"That will be quite enough of that. It's bad enough you must go to these matches without having to reenact them for me," Augusta protested.

Both of them looked at her, puzzled. Slowly,

enlightenment dawned upon Darnley's face. "Oh, I see! You're hipped about de Hasard." He dramatically looked toward the ceiling and lowered his voice. "About de Hasard," he added.

"Lydia passed us on the road, full of the news, you know. So her damned frog cousin took a flier, did he?" Billy asked, blinking at his sister. "Not at all certain that I want the blasted fop in my house. Hope you didn't put him in *my* bed?"

"No, of course not! I put him in my bed."

Darnley and the major were so clearly nonplussed that had Augusta been a little more in charity with them, she would have laughed. "What I mean is, he will lie in the paneled room and I will sleep in the red chamber. He says the mattress in his room—the paneled chamber is far more comfortable to his back."

"Well, I don't like it, not a bit," the major slurred, casting himself down in a chair and throwing one muddily booted foot over the arm. "Seems to me the fella's up to no good, as usual! More than likely, he's a bag of wind, and what he really means to do is steal the silver, or seduce the housemaids. Perhaps he's got his eye on Polestack!"

"More than likely," Darnley said, leaning negligently against the fireplace, turning his tulip glass in his hand. "Certainly had enough of the housemaids at the hall complainin' about him. Pinches on the staircase and such things as that." He shook his head. 'Damned loose fish," he added, hiccupping into his fist.

At that minute Mrs. Parrot, bearing a tray of nostrums for the invalid, entered the room. If she was shocked to find the two gentlemen having returned from a prizefight and very much in their cups, she gave no evidence of surprise.

"Good evening, Mr. Darnley, William. I apprehend that you enjoyed yourselves far more than we have this night," she said calmly.

"Heard about de Hasard's tragedy," Darnley said, effecting a clumsy bow in Mrs. Parrot's direction. He shook his head.

Mrs. Parrot's lips drew into a thin line. "It was a great shame, especially since he has managed to throw the entire staff into disorder." She looked down at the tray in her hands. "I thought some chicken-foot jelly and gruel would set him to rights."

"It always did us when we were small," the major exclaimed. "Perhaps you ought to lace it with castor oil."

Augusta, having had quite enough, stood up and shook out her wet skirts as best she could. "If all you can do is sit about in this odiously foxed manner, discussing a gentleman in the most vulgar terms, then I shall take my leave of you for the evening. I'll take the tray up, Mrs. Parrot. I can see you have had quite enough to do for one night. And, as for *you two*—well, I hope you are tortured by all sorts of blue devils tomorrow for speaking so ill of a very civil man."

With that she left the room and climbed the stairs, passing Crockett descending, shaking his head and talking to himself in no very pleasant tones concerning the demands of some people. "It is not at all what one is used to in a lady's household," he informed Augusta indignantly.

She knocked on the door of the paneled room and then entered, balancing the tray on her arm. "Monsieur de Hasard, I have brought you—" she started to say, then stopped, for the bed was empty.

For a moment, she blinked in the light of the single lamp on the bedside, but then she saw de Hasard, on his feet, wrapped in one of the major's dressing gowns, tapping on the ornately carved paneling.

For a long second they stared at each other, and then de Hasard seemed to recover himself. "I know, I know," he sighed. "You will reprimand me for being out of the bed, but even as I lie here, the most severe pain could not prevent me from examining the beauty of this fine old carving."

"Well, that is all very well and good," Augusta said, taken with admiration for his sense of beauty, "but it will do your back no good. Now, you must get between the covers and try to eat some of Parry's excellent jelly before you go to sleep."

He sighed, throwing up his hands, then

winced with pain as he obeyed her commands. Augusta placed the tray on the night table and smoothed the comforter over him. "Is there anything else you might want?" she asked, ready to ring the bell.

De Hasard grasped her hand and kissed it. "No, no, dear lady," he yawned. "Only to rest, if you please. In the morning I will feel very much more the thing, I promise you."

She shook her finger at him. "Only make certain that you do not try to get out of bed again tonight, *monsieur*. It is not a good thing for you!"

"Oh no," he sighed, closing his eyes. "I have taken a few drops of laudanum. I shall sleep like a baby tonight."

"Very well," Augusta said. "See that you do. Should you need anything in the night, you have only to ring."

He looked at her from beneath his eyelashes, the coverlet pulled up to his chin. "Oh, no," he said. "What I shall need, I shall be able to take care of myself."

15

As might have been expected, Miss Pole-stack was furious about the blue gown, and even more furious that she had been forced to move Augusta's things to the red chamber.

"And all for that Frenchman," she said as she brushed Augusta's hair, "who is no better than he should be, miss, you mark my words. I doubt that even naphtha will take the stains out of that gown," she grumbled. "And you coming in all soaking and wet, liable to catch your death of cold, and then where will you be?"

"I daresay I will be dead," Augusta said. Under normal circumstances, she would have wound the formidable Miss Polestack out of her sulks, but she was in no mood tonight to attempt such an arduous task, and Miss Pole-stack, who would have slept on a trundle bed on the floor rather than allow that Frenchman any opportunity of nocturnal wandering in her mistress's vicinity, eventually betook her-self off to the servants' wing with the ruined gown over her arm and a haughty sniff for a good night.

Augusta tumbled into bed and was very soon asleep, although it could not have been said that her dreams were pleasant nor her repose salubrious.

Any odd or unexpected noise in the night was enough to awaken her, and she heard Mrs. Parrot retire, and then the sound of her brother and Mr. Darnley bidding each other an inebriated good night, and the sound of the phateon's wheels and horses as they made their way down the drive through the mud.

After that, there must have been several hours during which she actually slept, however fitfully, for when she heard the sound of foosteps on the floor, her eyes flew open and she was instantly awake: she thought that she apprehended the figure she had first seen in the paneled chamber that night so long ago.

She sat up, reaching for the candlestick on the side of the bedstand as the shadowy apparition advanced upon her and she understood beyond all doubt it was the same figure. Before her fingers could close about the pewter stick, a hand had been clamped over her mouth and a strong arm was holding her captive.

"You will not scream, will you? I give you better sense," said Robert Darnley's voice as coldly sober as that of a curate.

Augusta, now more angry than afraid,

nodded violently and felt his hand removed from her mouth. "I was not aware, Robert, that your rights as a landlord included that of prowling about ladies' bedchambers in the middle of the—" she started to say, but his hand was clasped over her mouth again and the rest of her words were reduced to an unintelligible mumble.

"Will you listen to me?" he asked, and seeing she had no choice, Augusta nodded angrily.

"Alfred de Hasard is no more laid up with a bad back than I am drunk," Darnley whispered. "And his reasons for returning here from Paris are no more sentimental than yours or mine. The first thing he means to do is spirit Lydia away with him back to Paris—an elopement, if you will, although I doubt his intentions are as honorable as all of that."

"There was a time when you thought elopement a bad thing," Augusta said behind his hand, and he increased his grip slightly.

"Listen to me, my stubborn little ninny," he commanded in a hiss, "for there is far more to it all than just an elopement, although that is bad enough. She knows too much, and she doesn't know what she knows, and she *must* be protected! Will you help me?"

"Poor Billy, he loves her so—"

"Aye, he does, and when she sees what a great villain de Hasard is, she'll love him all the more. This man is dangerous. He's already killed once to achieve his ends. Do you recall the man in the phaeton accident at Sea Cross?"

Augusta felt a chill run down her spine and nodded.

"It was no accident. That man was a partner of de Hasard's, and de Hasard killed him. He is a dangerous man, Augusta, and a desperate one, for the man that he killed was in possession of certain papers that would have proved how deeply de Hasard *and* Lydia's father were embroiled in a scheme to sell information from the F.O. to Bonaparte's agents. I believe they were in a leather document case, and I believe de Hasard never found them."

Augusta began to shiver, but she could not talk.

"But there's no time to explain it all to you now. I only need to know if you can act quickly and quietly, and for God's sake, hold your tongue forever about this night's work—if we live through it."

"W-what do you want me to do?" she asked in a very small voice.

"Just as I tell you."

"But what about Lydia? Billy—"

"Your brother and Kirby are with Lydia. I've no doubt she'll rant and rave, but I think in the end, when she's told—well, just enough and no more—she'll see the light. Right now, you must come with me, and be very brave, Augusta—I know that you can be!"

"I'm in," Augusta promised. "Even though I do not understand at all."

"The less you know, the better right now," Darnley said grimly, squeezing her shoulders. "There's no time to dress. We must act quickly, if we are going to foil this monster's plots. Slip this riding cloak of Lydia's over your shoulders and put on your shoes."

Crawling out of bed in her nightgown, Augusta, moving as if she were in a dream, did as she was told.

"Now tie up your hair like Lydia's," Darnley commanded, and with trembling fingers, Augusta did so.

Darnley stepped back to survey the effect. He still wore the same clothes he had worn earlier that night, but she noted that there was a pistol thrust into the waistband of his trousers. He nodded his approval. "She's slightly taller, and you're heavier, but in the darkness, you can pass for her easily enough. Now come with me, and for God's sake, don't awaken anyone, or there will be hell to pay!"

He took her hand in his own and together they moved quietly down the length of the dark and silent hallway, past the closed doors, until they came to the paneled room. With his hand on the butt of his pistol, Darnley turned the knob and the door swung back silently on its hinges, the dim light from the lamp in the hall falling across the empty bed and a hollow darkness where the carved nymphs and satyrs had been.

"So that was why he wanted this chamber," Augusta whispered.

Darnley nodded. "It was an old priest's hole, from Cromwell's time," he said, advancing on it.

The opening was dark, darker than night, and a foul and stagnant air blew over their faces, far worse than anything Augusta had ever described in her novels.

"So, he found it, after all," Darnley muttered to himself, picking up the lantern from the night table and lighting it.

"It started as an old priest's hole, but when the smugglers—the Hawkhurst gang—were here, they made it into a tunnel. Used to store their cargoes of sherry and silk down in there. Come!" He took Augusta's hand and led her down the narrow, rotting wooden stairs into the hellish blackness.

Damp cold assailed her, and she drew Lydia's cloak close about herself, barely able to see more than a few feet ahead of herself, even with the lantern Darnley held aloft, uncertain where they would step.

But he seemed to know the way, and by holding tightly to his hand, she was able to make the long and steep descent. "It comes out under the old chapel at the hall," he said. "That's where de Hasard will expect Lydia to be waitng for him to whisk her away to Paris."

Augusta nodded, too uncertain to think.

"Listen, could you do a fair imitation of Lydia's voice?" he asked.

Augusta nodded again. "I suppose so," she said dubiously. "But why—"

"Come, then," he commanded. "I'm going to shield the light. We will be in total darkness, so you must trust me. Can you do so?"

"Yes," Augusta said in a very small voice. But something interesting was beginning to happen to her. Her fear was falling away, to be replaced by an odd, exhilarating excitement. For years she had written of just such adventures, and now she was about to have one herself. Tightly, she grasped Darnley's hand, and together they silently padded along the endless, winding corridors. It was, she noted, like a mine shaft, a tunnel dug out of the dirt and framed with huge timbers that, even in the darkness, she could feel were ancient and filled with rot.

Ahead—but how far she had no way of guessing—she saw a beam of light, and she squeezed Darnley's hand, gesturing toward it.

She felt rather than saw him draw the pistol from his waist, felt his lips against her ear. "Now," he whispered, "when I give the signal, all you must do is stand just out of the light and call out 'Alfred.' Can you do so?"

"Yes," Augusta said, and felt him urge her onward. Somehow, knowing that he was behind her with a pistol did not make her feel any less vulnerable as she stumbled over the rough dirt floor and felt the drip of water upon her head, running down her cheek like a tear, but she moved onward, her heart thundering in her chest and her palms moist with sweat, moving toward the light.

What she saw made her blink, her fear forgotten in amazement as she blinked into the pool of light that lay only yards away from her.

There crouched her supposedly invalided guest in a pool of lantern light, scooping, with both hands, piles of gleaming gold coins from a leather chest. The chest sat in a niche that might once have been an altar, its lid open like a mouth as the glittering gold poured out of it and into the hands of Alfred de Hasard.

But it was not the coins that drew and held her attention, pinned like a butterfly on cotton. It was the look upon de Hasard's face. It was as if a polite mask, a social role had been flung aside, as one would remove a cloak in the privacy of one's room, to expose the real person beneath the mask.

There was nothing either handsome or charming in the man who knelt, as if in worship, before the chest of coins; it was a skull upon which the face of greed had been molded by some sculptor. The chestnut eyes blazed with an awful lust, the lips were grotesquely drawn back from the teeth in a gargoyle's grin.

This, then, was the real Alfred de Hasard, she thought with an unexpected turn of nausea, a rage of betrayal, this grinning monster at worship over his gold.

How could she have been fooled? she

wondered. How could she not have seen? Was she so blind, then, so desperate for a man that she could have closed her eyes to this? She felt self-repulsion and doubt, and then, worse, a sort of fear that she could ever behold that light—that unholy light—in the eyes of a human being.

For what seemed like a very long time indeed, Darnley and Augusta stood in the shadows, watching as de Hasard scooped great, chinking handfuls of coins into the leather sack between his feet.

When Darnley squeezed her arm, she took a deep breath, calling herself back to the reality of the adventure at hand. Her voice sounded strange in her own ears as she called his name.

"Alfred!"

When he looked up at her, standing in the shadow of darkness, she knew she was not beholding the face of a sane man. As he instinctively thrust his body forward, covering the gold coins with his arms and chest, the look that seized his face was volpine, crafty and obsessed. It was several seconds before he could bring himself under enough control to arrange his features into the look of the de Hasard she knew, slowly straightening up, getting to his feet, reluctant to leave, even for a moment, the cache of gold.

"Ah, *ma petite Lydie*, there you are," he said in a voice that caressed, like a cold wind from a tomb caresses when first opened.

It took every ounce of her courage not to retreat from such a creature, not to turn and run from such madness.

Instinctively, she reached out behind herself, feeling for Darnley's presence, but her hands clutched only air, and she began, with a rising feeling of panic, to retreat from that hideous, advancing figure.

But she had taken no more than one step back when, behind her, she heard the old timbers supporting the roof of the tunnel beginning to groan, sagging beneath the great weight of the earth above, and she felt a trickle of dirt showering down upon her face and neck.

Startled, she moved before the Frenchman, her figure falling into the beam from his lantern, exposing her, not as Lydia, but as Augusta.

De Hasard laughed, the sound echoing through the darkened cavern, and from beneath his coat, she saw the metallic flash of a knife.

Before she could move, he was upon her, his arm locked about her throat, the gleaming point of the stiletto pressing into her flesh. He smelled hideously of mold and earth, as if he had been buried and risen again from the depths of hell. He was laughing, and the sound of it in her ears was ghastly, for it was not the laughter of a sane man.

"So, Darnley, you want to play games with me, hey? After so many years of eluding you and your kind, do you think that I have come this far and worked this hard to allow you to foil me now? Two years I have waited to retrieve this gold—two long, poor bitter years. And now you think this woman will stop me? You are a greater fool than I ever believed you to be. Indeed, you disappoint me." He spoke into the darkness, where nothing moved, save the sound of ancient timbers droning, and the soft, sibilant sound of ancient earth filtering down from the ceiling. "You see?" de Hasard cried, peering blindly into the darkness. "You see?"

Augusta made a sound as she felt the point of the knife pricking at her throat and the warm trickle of blood escaping from the wound. De Hasard laughed. "You think I would not kill her, or you or anyone else who stood in my way? I want that money, and I want *la belle Lydie* and no one can stop me now. No one!" His voice had risen to an hysterical pitch.

Augusta closed her eyes. She had written far too many heroines out of far too many similar situations to feel anything at that moment other than a deep and abiding sense of anger. Moving away quickly, she squirmed down in de Hasard's foul embrace and sank her teeth, as hard as she could, into his hand. She felt rather than saw the knife graze the side of her face, and had the satisfaction of tasting the blood of her enemy before she brought her heel up behind her and drove it into that area of de Hasard's anatomy in just the way Mrs. Parrot had always advised should she be faced with That Fate Worse Than Death.

De Hasard screamed, the sound echoing in the tunnel, and Augusta rolled from his deadly embrace across the dirt floor, just as Darnley sprang forward, his pistol in his hand.

Swift as lightning, de Hasard's bloody hand shot upward, knocking the weapon from Darnley's hand. As Augusta crawled across the floor in the darkness, groping for the lost pistol, the two men wrestled in the mud, locked in a mortal combat.

Augusta grasped the weapon in the dark and lay still for several long seconds, trying to discern which figure was that of Darnley and which that of de Hasard.

She had never fired a pistol in her life, and as she was attempting to pull the hammer back, it discharged.

The noise was deafening, and at first she thought it was the echoes of the bullet in the hollow tunnel. It was only when the earth began to crumble all around her that she realized the old tunnel was collapsing at last.

De Hasard's scream was the last thing she heard.

16

"I never knew you had it in you," Darnley said in a low voice as he toweled the mud and dirt from his face and hands in the library.

"Well, if I had waited for you to rescue me, I doubt very much if I would be alive to tell the tale," Augusta said, dabbing with spirits of ammonia at the scratch on her neck. "I think I could do with a drop of brandy—a very large drop of brandy," she added.

"Poor Crockett will come in in the morning and think what sots your brother and I must be," Darnley said, pouring her a glass and another for himself. "God, what a night's work."

"Where *is* Billy?" Augusta asked, sipping gratefully at the amber liquid.

"I would imagine he is consoling Lydia because her cousin failed to arrive and take her away to Paris. Good God, was there anything ever so ramshackle as that knave filling her head with the idea that she'd be the hit of Paris as his wife? I doubt he would have done much more than spirit her across the Channel before he'd squandered her inheritance and abandoned her to . . . Well, you may guess."

"Then his courtship of me was just a—a ruse," Augusta said, flushing with anger. "I simply cannot understand how Lydia could keep silent about such a thing."

"She can hold her tongue between her teeth when she needs to," Darnley said grimly. "Even when she was a little girl, de Hasard could wrap her about his finger. She always thought him fine as fire." He grimaced. "Which is part of the reason why no one save you and I must know what lies buried in that tunnel—de Hasard *and* his gold."

Augusta shuddered. "We were lucky. The beam that broke his neck must have weighed a ton."

"Don't think too closely. After all, he murdered at least one person to get at that gold. Let him lie there, where he can harm no one else."

"But all that gold!"

"All that cursed gold, bought with the cost of men's lives."

Augusta sat down wearily in a chair. The house was still, and only the clock in the hallway, ticking out the early-morning hours, made any sign of life. "Perhaps you'd better explain at the beginning. My head is spinning all about."

"Did you see those coins? They were new-minted eagles. French gold, Bonaparte's coin," Darnley said. He lowered himself into the sofa beside Augusta, closing his eyes with exhaustion.

"Ten years ago, when I left Niepert Garrison, it was to accept a government commission. I suppose you might say it was a sort of espionage, and the details of what I did are not very interesting now that the war is over."

"Oh, I would think—"

He laid his hand over hers and she was quiet. "One of the things that puzzled us a great deal was that Bonaparte's agents seemed to have a fairly good lead on certain bits and pieces of information that were coming from someone damned near the Prince Regent." He made a face of disgust. "Not that Prinny should have been trusted with *that* sort of tidbit to start with, but we began to feel that it was very possible someone in that rum circle was selling information to the French."

He sighed, sipping his brandy. "Now, at the same time, we were keeping our eye on certain young emigre bucks. Mind you, there were one or two who were damned tired of kicking their heels at Hartwell, and who yearned for *la belle France*, who could see that Bonaparte was offering them a lot more if they'd go back to France than they could ever hope for here, which has a certain honor to it, if you think on it for a time. But then there was another set, with access to information, who didn't mind selling it to Boney's agents. Not honorable."

"And de Hasard was one of those?"

"De Hasard and another young man—well, his name's not important now, he's from a good French family, and knowing what he'd done would only hurt them." He shook his head. "Now, you come to someone like my cousin—Lydia's father. Run off his feet, he was, and the estate, too. It must have been more temptation than he could stand when Cousin Alfred started telling him how much money he could make if he'd just repeat a little gossip."

"Lord Towson? Lydia's father?"

"Exactly so. Towson was selling information from the Prince Regent's dispatch boxes to his cousin de Hasard and the other fellow. The trouble was, he was family, for God's sake, and I thought I could put a stop to it that way. But he took his own way out—a header on the hunting field—and then the war was over. Well, he'd been paid, and paid handsomely, but in eagles, a coin he could no more spend in this country than American dollars, do you see? So, Towson and de Hasard stored it in the old smugglers' tunnel, waiting until the war was over, and I'll lay you a wager it came over the same way all those French wines and silks came in the war years, too, through the Hawkhurst gang."

"So de Hasard came back for the money. But what about the other fellow?"

"Well, the other fellow had a dispatch box or some sort of case full of documents that would have incriminated de Hasard as a traitor on either side of the Channel. It was his idea to blackmail him, and doubtless to blackmail Lydia, since they incriminated her father too. But fortunately de Hasard eliminated him for us."

"I guess we owe him that much," Augusta said, draining off her brandy. "Now can we open the dispatch box?"

"I don't suppose it can hurt anyone now," Darnley said, looking at the object on the table. With his penknife, he prized the lock and took a quick glance through the papers inside. Even Augusta recognized them as military dispatches, and she made a small disgusted sound in the back of her throat. "When I think that we almost lost Billy, and that he will limp for the rest of his life—" she said, and turned away. "Good God, what a night of horrors this has been!"

"I feel a sudden chill tonight," Darnley said, piling the papers upon the fire and watching as they curled and crackled into ash.

"We are best rid of them," Augusta said, drawing a shawl about her shoulders. "I am only glad that we are both alive."

"And that my poor cousin believes herself only jilted. But I am certain your brother will comfort her in that matter. There only remains the matter of you and I."

"You and I?" Augusta asked, glancing up from the fire.

Darnley nodded, all seriousness. "This is far too dark a secret to entrust to anyone outside the family. After all, if this became generally known, poor Lydia would be disgraced as a traitor's daughter. I am certain you would not want that fate for your future sister-in-law, would you?"

"My future . . . Do you really think? I mean, of couse they would deal very well together. If Lydia is a peeress in her own right, does that make Billy a baron?" Augusta asked wildly, taking a step back as Darnley advanced upon her with a purposeful tread.

"I was thinking of a more immediate method of ensuring your silence," Darnley said severely. "A more intimate way of connecting you to the family."

"If I wrote this as a novel"—Augusta laughed—"no one would believe it."

But she was able to say no more, for Darnley had taken her forcefully into his arms and was demonstrating the sincerity of his intentions in such a way as to leave her speechless, and quite happily so.

When at last she could speak, she gave a little giggle.

"What are you thinking now?" Robert asked her tenderly.

"How very, very improper Mrs. Parrot is going to find all of this in the morning."

"I would be inclined to guess that this was exactly Mrs. Parrot's intention when she brought you to Seaview Cottage. How little I shall worry about the future of our children with Parrot to guide them!"

"You are quite mad, Mr. Darnley," Miss Webb said, putting her face up for further proofs of this insanity.

About the Author

CAROLINE BROOKS is a practicing gerontologist who resides in Rising Sun, Maryland, with her husband and three children. Her interest in the Regency period was sparked when she purchased an old diary from that era in a Charing Cross bookstall during a visit to London in her student days.

INDIGO MOON

by *Patricia Rice*

bestselling author of *Love Betrayed*

*Passion ruled her in the arms
of a Lord no lady should love
and no woman could resist*

Lady Aubree Berford was a beautiful young innocent, who was not likely to become the latest
conquest of the infamous Earl of Heathmont, the
most notorious rake in the realm. But as his
bride in what was supposed to be a marriage-in-
name-only, Aubree must struggle to stop him
from violating his pledge not to touch her . . .
and even harder to keep herself from wanting
him. . . .